I0747554

Men of War

Bradley Poore

T. Willingham Publishing

Ann Arbor   Portland

For Linnea

CONTENTS

Men of War

A Movie? About Me?

When I was young there was a sitcom on NBC called *Wings*. The premise of the show isn't important for this story but the show's main characters were two brothers. One of the brothers was played by the actor Steven Weber.

"When they make a movie about your life, that guy from *Wings* should play you" a friend once told me. This was while the show was still on the air.

"Why would someone make a movie about me?" was my obvious response.

"You'll see, man. Just wait."

The only other time in my life when I can recall someone saying that specific phrase to me was when I was visiting my brother and his family many years ago. My brother's two boys were young, the oldest in elementary school and the other maybe in preschool. Both were glued to screens, the older one either playing video games or watching television and the younger one on an iPod Touch, which I think he was given for his fourth birthday, something I can still hardly believe. After arriving and going through the pleasantries that one does, I began to stare at his kids in amazement. I might have even scoffed a little. My brother picked up on this and said to me that very same thing: "You'll see, man. Just wait."

This was about my daughter, who had very recently been born. He was implying that this is how kids are raised these days and I should prepare myself for this inevitability. I, however, did not fall into this trap. I have purchased no gaming consoles, nor given my daughter free reign with a tablet, computer, or old phone of mine. If she does use them, it's only for audiobooks, which she can't get enough of. That has been chalked up to all the time she spent in the hospital after she was born prematurely; when we played audiobooks to her whenever her mom and I were there. We'd sit in her hospital room exhausted from our daily, and sometimes twice daily, visits. We had this mounting daily/weekly weight from not knowing the health of our daughter. We'd sit in nervous silence while listening to Stephen Fry read the Harry Potter books, our heads swiveling from her to the beeping machines above her bed, then gaze at the large window in our room. Looking out to the world below, the cars driving by, hoping none of these strangers had to experience what we were going through. Until a machine would beep, or a nurse would walk in, interrupting Stephen Fry and dragging us back to reality.

I did, however, purchase an arcade cabinet for a recent family Christmas gift, but one which only plays games from when I was a kid. This has been more interesting to me than anyone else in my family. No real surprise there. There has been some serious Dig Dug playing recently, though.

This movie topic did come up much more recently. Deep into my forties, I had picked up a second job. It had been decided that my daughter would attend private school, and the significant funds to pay for that school were somewhat in doubt. I found a position with an outdoor retail company, whose name boils down to three letters. I worked in the bike shop, following in my father's footsteps. I had no prior experience with bicycles, other than having one around for most of my life and listening to my father tell me stories of rear derailleurs, classic Bianchi 10-speeds, cassettes, down tube shifters, and many other bike-related things, which I am now just beginning to understand.

A couple of weeks into the job I walked into the bike shop part of the store where I worked, to hear one of the guys saying "If someone played you in a story of your life, which actor would you choose?"

I was floored. I think I stopped in my tracks when I heard that. With the constant music, the clicking of bicycle gears, and the overwhelming drone of all the fans running, no one even noticed I had walked back into the room, nor did they notice my gaping at the two of them. And without lending any more thought than being asked which he liked best, chocolate or strawberry milk, this person had an answer. He rattled off two actors, neither of which I had ever heard of, even after the guy elaborated on which movies they had been in.

This is something people think about? Amazing.

I have always found the conversation about the movie of *my* life curious. It took me longer to type the conversation out than it lasted in person, all those years ago. Why would my friend think anyone would want to make a movie about me, and my life? Also, we were in our late teens at that time. I had done so little, and lived a life that seemed so inconsequential—how could there even be enough for a short film?

My friend was not known to have premonitions of any sort. He knew not of tomorrow's weather nor the answers to his next algebra test. Where did he come up with this?

Did he know that years later, I would save that Sherpa's life while descending Everest? And I never did tell him about that time I was recruited by a three-letter government agency after I graduated college. But he *was* aware that during my short stint as a professional racing driver, I attempted to qualify for the Indianapolis 500, back in 2012. I even gave him that job as a producer on the kid's TV show I created years back.

Unfortunately, there were a few years there when we didn't speak after the deal with his sister. He ended up missing out on being called collect at all hours of the day and night as I cycled across Australia. I could have used his friendship while I was down there. I did feel so totally alone after the snake bite and subsequent coma.

I'm not sure if my life as a whole, or taken in parts, has been or is interesting enough for a movie. Sure, I've done a couple of interesting things throughout my life, but who hasn't? God, and don't even get me started on the time I fell off that damn cruise ship near Bermuda.

Can You Help Me Get My Car Out of That Field?

Have you ever wondered how an individual gets kicked off a demolition derby team? Of course, you haven't, who would?

This is a story about that very thing. On the surface, it's a bit of a head-scratcher. It's not a tale of undeniable failure, nor absolute triumph. Though it tips the scale toward failure. It's about the creator of a project, who finds himself removed from the very project he initiated. Though "project" is too formal of a term to label for a demolition derby, put on by a struggling town at their all but abandoned county fairgrounds.

How difficult is a project like this? How difficult is it to be a part of a group managing a project like this? If you are me, quite difficult.

Perhaps this is a tale of a fall from grace, without grace. Someone who thought differently and was ostracized from the sport he loved. I am being too dramatic, forgive me. Here is the tale.

I had what turned out to be another one of my terrible ideas. The event was a demolition derby, which at its core is a bunch of old, large American sedans and station wagons crashing into one another in a predetermined space, driven customarily by knuckleheads. I am counting myself and my friends among the members of this group.

When I dropped out of high school, I had a job at a local pizza and sub shop. Not to be confused with the other pizza and sub shop I've previously mentioned in my stories. Different place. The owner of the establishment decided to finally part with his 1977 Oldsmobile Delta 88. This behemoth was eighteen feet long and came equipped with a large V8 engine.

When he made an off-the-cuff remark about selling it for a mere $600, I jumped at it. I approached a few friends with the idea of using the car for a demolition derby, and a few came on board. I took up a collection, and the car was ours. A real bargain. The owner also felt it would be a fitting death to his long-time beloved car. Swift, and brutal.

The car was driven to my friend Tim's house, where the work would begin. According to the rules we'd picked up, there sure seemed like a lot of stuff to do to the car before the mid-August race. Race? Can it be called a race? Fracas? Melee? Debacle? Regardless, it was held every year in mid-August at the county fairgrounds near the edge of my town. So, rules in hand, "we" got to work.

Like most household DIY projects, the demolition turned out to be way more fun than the rebuild, but that's when the work ahead dawns on you.

Sample of the to-do list:
- Smash and remove all windows.

- Remove the stock fuel tank and replace it with a smaller, non-metal tank. The replacement tank needs to be bolted in place behind the driver.
- Relocate the battery inside the car.
- Weld vertical bars in front of the driver.
- Cut holes in the hood above the manifold in case of fire. Marshals need to be able to put the fire out. Foreshadowing.
- Bolt or weld the doors and trunk lid.
- Remove all seating (except the driver's).
- Paint a large number on the car.
- Weld a bar behind the driver's seat, seat post to seat post.

The list of items ranged from the easy to the "how the hell are we going to accomplish that?" It felt daunting to a bunch of teenagers with trivial automobile mechanical knowledge and few tools. At least, that was how it felt to me.

Having the car be at Tim's parent's house ended up saving our bacon. Next door lived a guy who participated in some amateur car racing, and he took a liking to our car. Well, bits of it. Turned out, the radiator that cooled the big V8 engine was so robust, he wanted it for his race car. In return for us letting him swap it out with a smaller one he had, he would also do all our welding, and all for free.

After the neighbor completed the work, we needed to move the car over to another friend's house. The demolition derby car had worn out its welcome at Tim's house. It was hauled over to a friend of ours named Ben, who would be piloting this piece of junk with reckless abandon in mid-August, forward and back, forward and back.

Over the next few weeks, the gas tank and battery were relocated, the seats removed, and the holes cut into the hood. Looking back, I don't remember being a big part of this work. I'm pretty sure my only contribution (other than being sometimes present) was in locating the car and coming up with the idea. As the project wore on, I became dead weight. Lacking any discernable skills, I could do little more than pick something up and move it here and there, or hand someone a wrench. This wouldn't stop me from soon putting everyone's hard work in jeopardy.

A few weeks before the demolition derby was to take place, I made an executive decision that the Oldsmobile 88 needed a thorough thrashing, a test to see if it could hold up to the rigors of the derby itself. So, on a lovely summer day, I got behind the wheel, bringing along another dispensable member of the team named Andrew.

Growing up in the country, the number of unpatrolled dirt roads seemed endless. I would take the car out for a drive, then bring it back unharmed, throwing in some fish-tailing for good measure. My whole life, I've had several members of my family engage in various forms of motorsports, but I was not one of them. My driving style would normally be characterized as "not overly aggressive."

Within five minutes of leaving Ben's home, I had firmly and enthusiastically planted the Oldsmobile 88 in a farmer's field, twenty feet from the road.

What did we do? We legged it. Back to Ben's house we went, with our tails between our legs. Andrew and I immediately jumped into my car and headed back to my neighborhood to go and talk to the one person I could always rely on, my oldest friend, Ronnie. Ronnie, who I'd watched fall through the ice when we were kids. Ronnie, who was riding his dirt bike with me on the back when he ran over a log on that trail, only to have it fly up and damn near tear his kneecap off. Ronnie drove a big-ass truck, which was quite capable of pulling the demolition derby car out of that field.

Amazingly enough, Ronnie was home and agreed to help out. He dropped whatever he was doing and grabbed a tow rope, and the three of us piled into his truck, setting off to recover the derby car and deliver it back to racing headquarters.

Unfortunately, upon arriving back to the field, we found a tow truck driver doing our job for us, with the farmer and a Michigan State Police officer to boot.

After spotting the police officer, Ronnie became uncomfortable with the situation he'd been roped into, so he turned down an adjacent road to drive us back to his house and send us on our way. We came across as undeniably suspicious, which led the officer to jump into his cruiser and pull us over. Ronnie was annoyed, the officer was annoyed, the farmer was annoyed, Andrew was silent, the tow truck driver didn't give a shit since he'd already hooked up the car, and I was left feeling like a complete idiot.

After approaching the vehicle and admitting that the car being pulled out of the field was ours, we were informed that to make this all go away, a fee of $100 would need to be paid to the farmer for the damage done to his field. This immediately took me back to the time two police officers had ordered my friends and me to pour beer they found in the trunk of our car over our heads. We *did* refuse, and the police agreed to let us pour them out on the side of the road. There always seems to be a gray area, if you look hard enough.

I wanted to feel like the local police were fleecing me, again. The farmer was in the right, and we did owe him something. In my previous encounter with the police, they were simply having a laugh but underestimated the white privilege standing before them. I was in the wrong now, and I damn well knew it.

Andrew and I only had $20 between us, so poor Ronnie was pulled deeper into this mess. Andrew and I gave our pittance to him, and he added his $80 and handed the money over to the officer. The officer let us know which towing company was hauling our car away, and he left our side to go give the farmer his recompense. More annoyed than I had ever seen him before, Ronnie drove us back to his house, and I promised to get him his money that day. I ended up having to turn to my mother to make up the difference, since the rest of the demolition derby team was pretty pissed off at me. And this only increased after I made the call to the towing company and got the price for the tow, plus daily storage of the car.

The car had to be retrieved, and this is the point in the story where my role in the team lessened. I was quietly fired for my stupidity. The team would go on without me. My last role would be to chip in on getting the car out of hock. After basically doubling the cost of the car, I truly deserved to be fired.

The car was retrieved, and the work was completed in time for the Lenawee County Fair in mid-August. I was allowed to get within shouting distance of the team and the car for race night. Kind of the guys. The car looked great, and Ben was strapped in and sent off to crash into other yahoos.

The tale that was relayed to the team after Ben drove off is as follows: The Olds 88 was magnificent. Ben was smashing and crashing and bashing into everyone and anything in his way. Until the fire. Ben said that he heard a loud bang from the engine compartment, and shortly after, a fire broke out under the hood. He tried to get the race officials' attention, and when that failed, he attempted to get out of the burning car. The race was halted, and the fire was put out by the officials. The Oldsmobile 88 was dead.

As for my old and dear friend, Ronnie, you'd swear I'd saved his life during some war, which led to some undying loyalty to me. There had been no war. I got him into far more hairy situations than he got me into. I think at the end of the day, we had been friends our whole lives, and *that* was enough. Out of all the kids who came and went in the neighborhood, Ronnie and I were the ones who were always there. We always had each other's backs. A bond never to be broken.

The Scrambler

This is not the multi-ingredient egg-based dish sold at your local greasy spoon. On the contrary, this is an organ-flipping, eye-crossing, hair-tangling, vomit-inducing, hit-you-in-the-head, and cause-you-to-get-stitches kind of amusement park ride.

As very few people know, I have a small scar on my forehead, near my hairline. I didn't see it myself for many years until a really bad haircut in my twenties, after which I had to shave all my hair off. And there it was.

"Oh, I remember getting this." I was speaking as much to myself as my live-in girlfriend, who was standing at my side a look of deep embarrassment on her face since she was the cause of the bad haircut, that had led to the shaved head.

"This makes me look tougher, right?" I asked her jokingly.

"Maybe if it was bigger?" she said sheepishly.

"Did I tell you this story?" I said, glancing over at her reflection in the mirror.

"I don't think so," she said with a shrug.

"It's from The Scrambler," I said with a smile. She just gave me a blank stare back. "You know, the ride at Cedar Point? It hit me in the head when I was a kid. Surely, I told you that story?"

"Did you?" was her only response. I could see the gears turning. She was starting to look bewildered. I then became lost in the memory as I stared at it in the mirror. I hadn't thought about that day at Cedar Point in so many years. I've told the story a few times, but it never causes as much astonishment as I hope, so I don't tell it much.

"Shit, I need to go to work. I'll tell you about it later, but that's pretty much the whole story." I then hurriedly got dressed and ran out the door.

I raced off to my social work job, which gave me too much stress and paid very little. I shouldn't complain too much—this is typical of many Americans' work experience. I am not foolish enough to believe my experience is unique. I felt like I was failing, at work, and in life in general. I had left the state I'd grown up in only to return in no better shape than when I left. The relationship with my live-in girlfriend was often rocky, and much of it was my doing. I was frustrated from spinning my wheels at my social work job which I was not very good at and I felt everyone knew that.

After my head was shaved, my work life improved slightly. My girlfriend's mishap with the scissors turned out to be a blessing in disguise. With my head shaved I came across as a wild card to the patients. At twenty-one, a skinny tall guy who wasn't going bald shows up with a shaved head people wonder, is there something wrong with this guy? Well, yes, plenty as it turns out. All of a sudden, I was unpredictable to the kids at the adolescent drug and alcohol rehabilitation center where I worked. It was the edge I needed. That thing that leveled the playing field for me with the patients. Those of us who aren't blessed with brawn and intimidating personalities need to manufacture it in other ways.

That first day after the initial shock wore off, I tried the Cedar Point story out on a couple of my coworkers.

"Do you see this scar?" I'd say to them, pointing up near my hairline with a big grin on my face. This would lead to an awkward lean-in on their part, and some squinting.

"Um, yeah, I guess so?" they'd respond in kind.

"Cedar Point!" I'd exclaim. "The Scrambler? You know, the ride?" This was where I would take both of my hands, put them out in front of me, and start swirling them in a horizontal movement as if my hands were brushes and I was washing the hood of a car.

"Ahhhhh," was the most likely response I would get after that hand show. "That's where you got that? At Cedar Point?" This would then allow me to tell the tale.

"I was hit in the head by a ride at Cedar Point when I was a kid. It was called The Scrambler." I'd also throw in the mimicking of the door swinging open and striking me in the head. This resembled me slapping myself in the head with the palm of my hand. After this, I would start to lose people, so I would next throw in a few other details that I still remembered.

"Wow," was the best response I could have hoped for at this point in the story.

"You know what else, I got to ride in the Cedar Point ambulance. Okay, well, it's a golf cart," I'd finish off slyly.

"Where did they take you, to the Cedar Point hospital?" was the typical response.

"They did!" I'd say enthusiastically. "I had to have a couple of stitches put in." I'd point up to my scar again with a dramatic flair.

There wasn't much to say after that, and the story normally petered out. No, I didn't receive a lifetime pass to Cedar Point for my injury. I didn't even receive a pass for the summer, that I know of. Even if we had, my parents weren't too keen on the place after that happened. I mean, I went to an amusement park hospital, got a couple of stitches, and was chauffeured around in a golf cart. How is that not a good story?

There was another time in which the story didn't elicit the reaction I had hoped for. Again, during my social work career, I was late to work one day because a single-engine plane was forced to make a landing on the median of the highway. Sure, I didn't see the thing land on it, but I had driven by shortly after. When I strolled into work late with what I considered a pretty dazzling story, I couldn't wait to see the look on their faces.

"Wow, that's amazing, Brad," they would say.

"A plane on the highway? No way," I'd hear.

But there was nothing. Maybe it was because I played it cool and didn't put a lot of flailing hands and emotions into the tale. It fell quite flat.

A little while later, a coworker of mine came into work and I heard him telling the same story that I had told just a short time before.

It was as follows: "Sorry I was late, traffic was crazy, and there was a small plane in the median of the highway."

"Oh my god, no way!" I heard one of the same coworkers I told the story to say.

"I told you guys that same story earlier," I blurted out as I walked up into their conversation.

"You did?" came back at me from at least two of the people I'd spoken with earlier.

This now lends itself to the story of Michael Collins, best known as the loneliest man in history. Michael Collins was the astronaut who stayed in orbit above the moon while Buzz Aldrin and Neil

Armstrong went down to the surface. At that point, Collins was the farthest any one person had been away from any other living soul.

A pretty heavy-handed awkward analogy, yes. This is what I am going with. Perhaps if Collins would have made the trip down to the surface of the moon alone, checked things out, came back up to the ship, and let the guys know everything was okay, then Aldrin and Armstrong received all the glory, conceivably the analogy would work.

My point is, this was just one of the examples of a time when I was seeking a little glory but failed to find it. My audience was just not listening.

So, back to The Scrambler; let me sum up here. I was a kid at Cedar Point amusement park, maybe six-ish, or seven-ish. My older brother and I went to get on a ride called The Scrambler. We had entered the area after the ride had stopped but before the previous riders got out of the cars. When the previous rider swung the door open to exit the car, it hit me in the head. I was then taken by a Cedar Point branded ambulance golf-cart-type vehicle to the park's hospital. I received two to three stitches on my head, and I still have a small scar. I never did get to ride The Scrambler, and I'm sure we went home after I received my stitches. A trip to the amusement park was ruined, and I lived to tell the tale.

If you ever hear this story at a gathering, we are both attending, act surprised and enthusiastic, and then ask me about Michael Collins, who stayed up on the ship while those other two fuckers got all the glory. You try steering a spaceship for more than three seconds and let's see if you don't crash the thing. I'm not calling myself a hero here, but you can.

Doctor, We Need You

There were times in my early teens when I did things so out of character they still feel like some silly sitcom or sketch comedy bit. Things that were brazen, reckless, and most importantly, stupid. Much of it fell into a category that if done in *any* of the fifty states would be illegal.

I will spin the wheel and choose something at random. Maybe take the time I went to our local hospital and wandered the halls. Sounds harmless, you'd think. Just a bored kid with not much on his plate for the day, killing time. But let's now throw in the fact that I was there for a specific reason, and I wasn't *just* walking the halls but also entering rooms, offices, and supply closets. The funny thing (at least to me) was that I wasn't seeking drugs. I was smart enough to know that drugs weren't left out in the open, no matter how poor my opinion of our local hospital was. I considered the hospital mildly negligent for things I'd seen done since childhood, but nurses leaving medication out in the open seemed beyond that scope.

Why would I do it then? Boredom, sure. Stupidity, you bet. A burning desire to take risks, yep. Did I mention stupidity? I was on the hunt for one specific medical device: a defibrillator. Okay, I admit that would make for a better story, but it's not true. Can you imagine a bunch of thirteen-year-old boys crowded around the thing in some basement, daring each other to be the first one to try it? I would not have been the first. Maybe the second, but not the first. No, I was on the hunt for hemostats. One, two, or a whole case of them. I would have considered finding one a huge victory.

This was the time in my life when I first became obsessed with smoking weed, and a necessary tool in your weed toolbox was certainly a nice pair of hemostats. Yes, small alligator clips would work, but I would have found it awkward to walk into my local Radio Shack and just buy a set of alligator clips. A little too on the nose, even for thirteen-year-old me.

These good-quality medical-grade hemostats were a rare find amongst the young pot-smoking-elite and to get a pair with the bend at the end was unheard of. You essentially had to be a doctor's kid and swipe a pair when your old man wasn't looking, then sell them to the highest-paying stoner. There was a rumor once that they even came in a lovely gold color, but such a white whale was never seen by my eyes. Even a straight pair would have elevated my status, and if we were able to acquire enough, this would make for a good side-hustle.

"Hey man, do you have any left?" a kid at school would quietly ask in the hallway in between classes.

"A few," I'd slyly reply, opening my trench coat to reveal pairs of dangling hemostats, clipped to the inside of the coat, neatly arranged by size. "How many do you need?" I'd say with a smirk.

But as hard as I tried and as many days as I walked the halls of the hospital, dashing in and out of rooms, peering through windows and checking for doorknobs that would turn, it was not meant to be. I could have snatched gauze and Band-Aids all day long, but what did a stoner need with those? Nothing. It was always going to be in the next room, or that next doorknob would be unlocked to reveal the jackpot. It was a bust. There would be no joyous celebration the next day at school, where the other stoners would hoist me up onto their shoulders and carry me all of six feet before getting too winded and putting me down. My increased status would be on hold, indefinitely.

Later in life, I would think of those days after pulling a plastic pair of hemostats out of my daughter's play doctor kit, or when I'd come across alligator clips in some computer repair kit at work.

"No teenagers work here," I would mutter before pulling them out and examining them for any burn marks near the opening. Habit, if I had to guess.

I recall watching the show *ER* in some teenage disbelief as they would seemingly go through a hundred per episode. Did they have a problem with hemostats disappearing from their set? How could they have not? Another reason to be disappointed I never entered the entertainment business. I could have finally achieved that side-hustle, though I think that term has recently been rebranded as "over-employed."

The only side-hustle I could manage was chewing gum while walking. No, that's making light of my abilities. I once recall a time when I was walking to a restaurant downtown where I now live, dealing with a work issue on the phone, and smoking. Yes, all at the same time. A big pat on the back for Brad!

Goodbye Scuba Guy

Throughout my childhood, my maternal grandparents owned a cottage near the western shore of a small lake in Michigan called Devil's Lake, named after Robert Devil, Sr., who purchased the lake and surrounding eight hundred acres of land from Henry Walter and his family on January 2, 1900. The Walter family believed the lake was cursed, so to combat this, monthly Pagan sacrifices were held, ever since their eldest son Max drowned in that lake in 1889.

The highly superstitious Walter sold the whole 1500 acres (800 acres of land plus the 700-acre lake) for $1,889. The Walters, ask for this particular amount of money because it corresponded with the last year their eldest son inhabited the earth.

Robert Devil, Sr. had gone from pauper to prince via a lucrative government contract, supplying saddles and wagon wheels to the US Army during the 1880s. Before the century was over, Devil would become even wealthier via the Spanish-American War, which broke out in August 1898, further adding to his already-bulging war chest.

Devil, Sr. had increased his wealth even more by dividing up and selling plots of land around the lake in the early 1900s. The wealthier Americans were beginning to purchase vacation homes, partly as a means to shelter themselves from a tax-happy government. Devil took advantage of the last few years he was alive, securing his wife and children's future by selling off the parcels. Devil, who was a shrewd businessman and pillar of his growing community, ended up drowning in the very lake which bore his name in 1911 after falling through thin ice while checking on a fishing trap. He was sixty-seven.

My grandparent's cabin was located on the western side of the lake near the Devil's Lake Yacht Club. I would spend a lot of my summer weekends there, either swimming in the lake, riding around on their pontoon boat, or marveling at the drunken antics of my father, my uncle, and my uncle's friends. As it happens, one of my uncle's friends, who went by Stinky Pete or Dickhead or some such nickname, had a speedboat named *Jaws*. I remember drunken tales of how *Jaws* was the most feared boat on the lake. Honestly, the one time I saw the boat on the lake under its power, it was twenty yards from its dock, backfired a few times, and subsequently broke down. It lived up to its name, since I'd since read the mechanical shark in the movie was a piece of junk too.

On a beautiful summer's day at the cottage, I watched as Dickhead walked straight through a closed sliding glass door. Blood was everywhere. Dickhead was swiftly whisked off to the nearest hospital for medical treatment. The fact that your blood thins as alcohol is consumed contributed to the gore left splattered all over the patio. Dickhead *did* survive, and hopefully, he learned a valuable life lesson. Alcohol and glass doors don't mix? Not sure that is an actual life lesson, but there has to be something there.

Another thing I loved as a child was celebrating my birthday at the cottage. My birthday falls in mid-August, and it's the perfect time to be out there on that lake. For my eighth birthday, we again made this trip out to the cottage to spend it with all the family. It wasn't the birthday that drew the family out, it was the free lodging and watersports. For my birthday that year, I received a red-suited toy scuba diver. He was around ten inches long, plastic, and battery-operated. When turned on, it would kick its flippered feet and swim along the surface of the water. It was fantastic. A battery-operated toy that you could play with *in* the water? I was in awe. The scuba tanks held four-C-batteries, which were only good for a few minutes of scuba-ing. It's hard to say if this was the poor quality of batteries in the 1980s or how inefficient battery-operated toys were back then. Both, maybe.

Even though it was my birthday, my older brother also received a scuba guy to play with. His was blue. This was something many parents would do, try to make life fair. Siblings always receive the same number of Christmas gifts, and in my family, birthdays were also in play. Teaching children that life is fair feels contradictory to what they will encounter later in life. The university they have to attend doesn't accept them, that job they are perfect for doesn't hire them, their parent's divorce, and yes, their brother or sister will get a gift and they will not. Disappointment *cannot* be avoided, only postponed.

Without sabotage by my hands, my brother's scuba guy stopped working after one day. No, I did not weaken or removed the rubber seal which surrounded the battery compartment, it simply stopped functioning. Did stores even take things back in those days? Even with the manufacturing shift to Asian countries like Japan and Taiwan, toys were produced to a much higher quality than they are today. At least this has been my experience.

With our time at the cottage running out, for some reason I became sentimental about my scuba guy. My red scuba guy would soon be heading back to dry land, his scuba vacation coming to an end. Back to his day job, relegated to being used in the bathtub in our small home, then to the toy bin to get shuffled to the bottom and more importantly have his batteries corrode inside his scuba tanks, ruining him forever.

A better ending for this fine athlete was to live out his days swimming across Devil's Lake. This would be his swimming of the English Channel or his Cuba-to-Miami swim for freedom. This would be the final one-way trip for Red Scuba Guy.

So, on the last day of our trip, I inserted new batteries, took a swim to the edge of the shallows, turned on Red Scuba Guy, laid him in the water, pointed him toward the middle of Devil's Lake, and gently let him go. Red Scuba Guy was free, or at least until his batteries wore out, or he was obliterated by a drunken boating enthusiast.

I watched my new friend swim off into the distance, through the tiniest of wakes created by long-gone pontoon boats crammed with families seeking an escape from their weekly doldrums. I would never forget those few days surrounding my birthday when I was given the greatest of toys at the most opportune time. As he swam off to the unknown, I hope he too shed a tear for the friend he was leaving behind.

A postscript to this story:
Three decades later, my brother still owned Blue Scuba Guy. He fixed the small gear that had broken all those many summers ago at the lake, then sold him for $125 on eBay to a man who lived in Hawaii.

Have You Given Any Thought to Hell?

Well, have you? Have you given this some thought? I'm not just proposing a rhetorical question to drive my story or a one-sided tale. Stop reading for a second and dust off the old mind movie projector. Throw it up on the screen and think about it. I am about to tell you my version—you should do me that favor.

So, have you? Last chance. What I am getting at is the fate of Sisyphus, who was forced to roll a boulder up a hill for all eternity. Well, sort of. Sisyphus didn't receive this punishment from Hades because of some bouldering misdeeds in life. This was a symbolic punishment. I propose to take this a little farther, though. A more tailored experience if you will. A tailored experience for you, the damned.

Let's go over this, shall we? You spend your college years waiting tables, and maybe you're *really* bad at it. You drop trays laden with food in the last few steps before getting to the customer. You get caught and then subsequently fired for looking down a woman's dress instead of taking down her order. Maybe this is your hell, and you are stuck waiting tables for eternity.

Maybe you have agoraphobia and are forced to endlessly attend football games in stadiums filled with drunken, screaming assholes. Is that something anyone can get used to, agoraphobia or not?

Are you thinking of yours? Take a moment. The book will wait.

Go on to the next page when you're ready.

Ideas:

A woman I once dated was once a victim of date rape. Ideally, her attacker's hell would find himself being penetrated throughout eternity in any number of horrifying and clever ways. A deserved fate one could argue.

A selfish, childless couple who spends all their disposable income traveling the world and outwardly mocking everyone from their social media accounts on how wonderful and fulfilling their childless lives are. Maybe they get stuck on an endless flight with screaming babies in every other seat. Or perhaps they are foster parents to ten children who financially, emotionally, and physically drain them for eternity.

If you hated school, are you stuck attending classes forever? Listening to someone cut their nails? It can't be as easy as having to go to the dentist every day to get work done. That feels too broad. Again, Sisyphus didn't kill a petrologist while alive to then be forced to fuck with rocks his whole life. Maybe you were a bad person – oh, I don't know, let's say you were an arsonist, and one of the things you hated in life was boats because you get seasick. Sticking you on a boat for eternity does not correlate with your burning shit, it's just punishment specifically designed for you.

Sorry, I am going on and on here. What about me, you're probably thinking? This *is* something I've given thought to. If I lead a dishonest, unmeaningful life, what might I be forced to do for eternity? What's my hell?

It's a dueling piano bar filled with women, all having their fortieth-birthday parties. I have been trying to work in the raking of leaves somehow, but I just can't do it. We could make it an outdoor dueling piano bar, in Michigan, in the fall, and my job is to rake leaves, and listen to terrible music, forever.

Hell isn't just a punishment for the stranger you didn't feel like helping that morning on the way to work, the unforgivable deed you committed, or that secret you dare not tell even to your closest friend. Hades knows what you hate, and knows that one thing that grinds your gears. He knows you've stolen money from your child's piggy bank for beer; knows you groped a woman at that Lollapalooza in 1994. Hades, or whatever you want to call him/her/them, will use all your misdeeds against you and love every second of your torment.

Perhaps our paths will cross down there while we're mowing a lawn, shoveling snow, jumping rope for eternity, or sitting through every black-and-white movie ever made. If so, say hi, will you?

Men of War

Over several years, my friend Tim and I have had this shared hobby of taking pictures of strange and interesting signs and then emailing or texting them back and forth. The original idea was to create a funny picture book one day, but we were so bad at keeping track of all the pictures taken that most have been lost, be it through a computer crashing or just negligence on our part. While we've lost track of the overall point as the years ticked by, we still find ourselves taking pictures of odd street signs, poorly spelled signs on public bathroom doors, and any stupid sign that make us laugh. Now and then, a story can be told to narrate one of these pictures. And in rare cases, the story is better than the picture.

We liked road trips as teenagers. This isn't unusual, because when many teens get their driver's licenses, it's all their parents can do to keep them at home and not just driving around. These were the early 1990s, and gas hovered around $1.00 per gallon. Taking a driving trip in a small car was an easy decision, it seemed so trivial to do a trip from Michigan to a place like Florida for less than $75. We were young, so there was also no wasting money on a hotel stay on the trip down. Swap out the driver, take a nap, repeat.

So, during summer break, with little, well, probably no planning, in our seventeenth year on this earth, my friend Tim and I headed south, to Florida. I had grandparents living in Sarasota at that time, and I knew we could get a free night or two out of them as we planned our next destination. I had my mother give them a call after we headed out. It would be a diet of Mountain Dew in glass bottles, 100 Grand candy bars, McDonald's, and Winston brand cigarettes for the next week. Cigarettes were a bargain in some of the Southern states, so that was worth the trip. Friends were always clambering for $10 cartons of cigarettes. That also meant everyone was happy to see you upon returning home.

After arriving in Sarasota, we received a call from a girl named Nicole, whom Tim was casually dating. She and a friend had also driven down to Sarasota and wanted to hang out. After joining up with the two gals, we hung out for a day or two in Sarasota. Then someone pitched the idea to drive down to the Keys. I was game, but in agreeing I knew I'd lose my travel companion. The girl he was dating had a very expensive convertible, which she offered up for him to chauffeur the two of them down to the Keys. I ended up having her friend ride shotgun with me, and neither of *us* was happy about it. I didn't blame him, it was a tough thing to pass up.

The females are just extras in this story, bit players. They serve as shadowy scenery but played no role in the overall narrative. After staying in Key

West for a night or two, they packed up and headed back to Michigan. I don't think I saw either one of them again.

Tim and I then spent a little time exploring the island and then the adjacent Keys as we drove back up the long bridge toward the Florida mainland. At one particular stop near the ocean, we parked the car and strolled down to the beach, just to look out at the ocean. As soon as we hit the mainland, we might not see the ocean again on this trip. We were standing there, just a few feet apart, and as I gazed out at the ocean, I heard Tim speaking. I heard.. something.

"Portuguese…" I thought I heard. Followed by, "Men of war,…" then "On the beach."

It took a second to sink in. Then I spun my head to look at him in surprise.

"What did you say?" I spluttered to Tim.

"What?" Tim said, looking back in confusion.

"Fucking men of war, coming out of the ocean?" My head spun back to stare out at the water in disbelief. I didn't see them. Where were they?

"And didn't you say they were Portuguese?" I searched left, then right, seeking a glimpse of these men of war. Panic was starting to set in.

"That's fucked up," I said, mesmerized by the ocean, daring the men of war to pop their heads out of the water, again. Supposedly.

"What the hell are you talking about?" Tim's voice barely broke through my sweeping, panicked stricken-gaze.

I rounded on him in desperation, "You said army men from Portugal were going to come out of the ocean." My gaze swung back to the ocean, which without a doubt would now be teaming with army men from Portugal. We sat in silence for a few seconds as Tim tried to regain some composure and straighten me out.

"Portuguese man o' war," he said slowly, fighting back a giggle.

"Yeah, I know." I began growing increasingly frustrated by his dulcet tone and was now glaring at him. Then I noticed it. His arm. Tim was pointing over my shoulder but not at the ocean, but rather to a sign near the edge of the beach. A sign that had only been several feet from us the whole time.

No, it was not a warning sign with a picture of a soldier coming out of the ocean—it was a warning sign with a picture of a long-tentacled sea creature: a Portuguese man o' war.

In an instant, my terror and frustration with Tim slid effortlessly into abject embarrassment. Tim was now in fits, practically doubled over in hysterics at my stupidity. How could you blame him? I always played the fool so well.

No Portuguese army men were coming to get me. No attack was imminent on this stretch of Florida beach. I did not need to run and get my Swiss Army knife out of the car for protection, and once again it was simply me, not understanding life. Like many times before when I rushed to judgment before knowing all the facts, misread a sign which then led me astray, or didn't push the correct button after getting into the elevator. I drive past roads, entrances, and driveways that are marked. I have embraced who I am and what function I need to play in life. Sometimes things go wrong; other times I sail through the red light, unscathed.

All the signs Tim and I have taken pictures of over the years are no different, read but seldom understood. We snap pictures because we are bewildered, because the signs have dirty or misspelled words, and sometimes we take a picture to find out later we're the idiot, not the sign-maker. I use the word "we," but clearly, it's "me."

I like to think of this as a cute quirk, just part of my personality, not the terrible annoyance I'm sure it is.

My Friend, Dustin

I was twenty-five years old when I found myself staring at the back of a teenage patient, his swinging legs dangling over the side of the hospital's rooftop.

He appeared to not have a care in the world, as if he were waiting up there for a lunch date with an old friend.

Management chose me for this job. Me. "You're the only one he's bonded with," Charles, the head of the unit told me after we hit the final staircase landing before we opened the door and I was sent out on my own to deal with Dustin, who by my estimate had now been out on the ledge for around twenty minutes already. One minute, twenty, an hour, what did it matter? Dustin was still out there on the ledge, and not on the pavement nine stories below.

Dustin came to us as a ward of the state. He was two months shy of his sixteenth birthday when he was admitted to our unit. That was almost five months earlier. Dustin had attempted suicide while in foster care—pills. Over the proceeding months, Dustin had been a patient whom we'd all done our best to glean information about from a variety of sources, to understand his past and present mental health. According to his last foster parents, Dustin had been abused as a small child by his biological mother. His mother never wanted children and let this be known to Dustin, who seemed to still carry that memory from childhood. We didn't know his mother's name, and never would.

Dustin's mother (or who the police believed was his mother) dropped him off at a police station when he was six.

The desk sergeant's notes were as follows:

An unidentified woman and a male child walked into the Barnard St. entrance to the police station at 1:10 pm on Tuesday, June 10th. The unknown female walked up to Sgt. Avery and stated, "I am no longer going to care for this child. His name is Dustin."

The mother then turned around and walked out of the station. After exiting the station, she was then briefly seen heading north on Barnard St.

Patrolman Capinski walked over to Sgt. Avery and asked about the exchange they just had. After being informed about the situation, Patrolman Capinski exited the station and attempted to locate the woman. She was not located.

The remainder of the desk sergeant's notes remains inconsequential.

Dustin bounced around foster homes, mostly due to anger-related outbursts. Some of the families knew his background, some didn't. Either way, the abandonment he felt as a child continued into his teens, and in the end, led him to our facility.

This could be considered Dustin's second attempt, but I believed if this attempt were acted upon, it would be his last, and final. The first suicide attempt had initially been labeled a mix-up of medications and *not* intentional. After being at our center for several weeks, Dustin had confided in me that it had been on purpose but may have only been a half-hearted attempt.

Dustin was a good actor—with his life, he needed to be. After some time in the unit though, I felt he was being honest, and not being misleading just to gain sympathy from me, or the staff.

At times, he also spoke of the physical abuse he had suffered at the hands of his mother, but the other staff and I wondered if these were actual memories he was recalling or memories falsely created through so many years of intense mental health treatment. He talked about being left alone for long periods, possibly even days. Abuse, from my perspective, seemed likely.

We believed that Dustin grew up in a somewhat rural setting, but again, no one knew how accurate this information was since no family member could ever be located and the authorities could find no missing person reports fitting Dustin's description. Where he was born or even what city he and his mother lived in had never been identified. Also, no DNA profile had ever been found to be a match to his, in any database. Dustin was discarded by the one person who should have loved him.

I turned away from Charles to look down at the horizontal steel bar that would lead me onto the roof. I could see a crack of light through the opening. I heaved a heavy sigh, and with Charles on my heels, I pushed the bar and went onto the roof.
"He's on the east side, right in the middle," Charles whispered behind me.

I weaved my way around a huge rooftop air-conditioning unit that was howling like a jet engine before takeoff. Then I spotted him.

Dustin was exactly where Charles had said he would be. I stood thirty feet directly behind him and, for a moment, just watched. Dustin's legs were gently swinging, his heels bouncing off the side of the building. He was dressed the same as when I saw him a couple of hours ago: plain white T-shirt, jeans, and his blue low-top Converse All-Stars. His black hair was being blown skyward by the relentless gusts that climbed up the side of the building. He did seem at ease.

I decided to slowly approach to get within non-shouting range. When I got to around twenty feet from him, I decided to speak.
"Hey, Dustin."

I went with a low-key monotone greeting, as if we were a couple of high school acquaintances passing each other in the hallway in between classes. I stayed at twenty feet, waiting for a sign that he'd heard me. His feet still swayed and bounced off the wall.

With all the wind and noise from the street below, did he hear me? My voice tends not to carry very well, either. I kept my tone steady and tried to raise it above the din.
"Hey, Dustin?"

Feet still swinging, he raised his right arm above his head in a "hey, over here" sort of wave. It stopped as quickly as it had begun though.

"Can I come over? Not too close," I added quickly, and then immediately regretted my backtrack.

Dustin held up his left arm and raised his index finger. Guess he was thinking it over.

"Do you mind if I keep talking?"

A pause, then a small shake of his head. Left to right.

"I'm going to come a little closer and sit down. It's noisy up here and if I have to keep yelling, I'll lose my voice."

I halved the gap between us and sat crossed-legged on the rocky tar roof. Later in life, I would look back in amazement at how I could ever sit like that, and more importantly, how I ever thought I could do this kind of work.

I spun around to see Charles, who was now joined by Darshan Singh, our hospital VP, his minion Sandy, and another well-dressed woman I didn't recognize. After scanning the group, I looked at

Charles and raised my left hand toward my mouth with my first two fingers extended into a V shape, which signified I needed a cigarette. After a nod from Charles, I gestured toward the roof with my finger and then made a motion with my left hand as if I were opening the left side of a jacket to reveal the inner breast pocket. As I pointed with my right hand at the invisible pocket in the left side of my jacket, Charles again nodded, then turned and left. If he spoke to the others before leaving, I didn't hear. I had ridden my motorcycle to work that day, and my cigarettes still lay in the inside breast pocket of my leather jacket, which today would commonly be taken up by a cell phone. Charles had taken enough breaks with me over time—he would find them.

I turned back toward Dustin.

"So, how the heck did you get out here?"

Start with the light-hearted approach, I thought. I came off this way to most patients, so it shouldn't seem disingenuous to Dustin. And after all, I was curious. Our third-floor adolescent psychiatric unit was typically well shut; escapes were not normal. To my knowledge, a patient leaving the hospital hadn't happened prior, and no one had gotten onto the roof.

Dustin shifted his weight a few inches to the left so he could speak to me better.

"The door to reception," he said with just a hint of a smile.

"We were going to lunch, and I saw the window inside the lobby had been left open. I checked the door and it was unlocked."

"After that, I found the stairway that led out, or to the roof. I decided to go up. The door to the roof was unlocked."

He turned back to face the world, still muttering something I couldn't hear. I tried hard to read his lips as he turned.

"It was meant to be." But that took me years to come to terms with. I still want to deny it. To remember it differently.

It wouldn't have mattered that day if it

had registered, or not. It wouldn't have changed the outcome.

My mind was racing. Being up here was already sensory overload for me—Dustin, and this mess, the wind, the noise, the height. I was in damn near panic mode.

"Hey, I sent Charles down to grab my smokes. When he gets back, do you want one?"

Keep him talking. Keep him talking.

Dustin gave a little shrug, followed by a gentle nod of his head.

Where the fuck is Charles?

"You scared the hell out of a lot of people running off like this. I was worried."

I gave it a few seconds to see if I could merit a response but was met with silence.

"I thought you might be on your way to Key West?"

And that time, I may have gotten a smile. If I could keep him talking, actually get a dialogue going, then just maybe he'd remember all those times he sat at his desk in the room with me on the edge of the bed, talking. We spent a lot of hours like that. The goal with any patient was trust. He trusted me enough to tell me how he gained access to the roof, so that was something.

There were times you might pull open the window, allowing them to see into your life. Just giving them some inconsequential piece of you that if put under a microscope would be meaningless. But to the patient, you could become more than just an authority figure—maybe a confidant, or a friend.

Dustin had told me of a memory that he believed to be true. When he was a child in his mother's care, the two of them took a trip to Galveston, Texas. He sat in my office, staring out the window as he recounted this. He told me his memory of the downtown area and how the cruise ships were moored nearby. Of course, he would have been a small child and couldn't give me enough detail as to when this took place or how long it might have taken to travel there. It was a curious memory, but it gave no insight into his past.

"Brad," I hear from behind me.

Charles was now standing several feet back, cigarettes and lighter in his right hand.

"Hey Dustin, Charles is back. He's going to give me my cigarettes and then leave us be. Okay?"

Not taking my eyes off Dustin, I motioned with my left hand for Charles to approach. I could only hear every other footstep on the gravelly roof over the noise. I held my left hand out, palm up, and Charles laid the lighter and cigarettes in it. The weight was more than I expected it should be, and it shifted in my hand before I closed my fingers around it. It was a beautiful antique Dunhill lighter—a gift from a college girlfriend who knew of my love for all things art deco. She used to tell me I was born in the wrong era.

I warmed inside and thought of her every time I looked at it, that day was no exception.

I took a quick peek in the box—nineteen left. I'd picked this pack up on my way to work and had one between the bike and the entrance to the hospital. If I was up here a while and splitting these between two people, they wouldn't last long. Before coming up here, I knew Dustin smoked, and I also know we smoked the same brand. *Small details can sometimes matter*, I thought.

I pulled two out of the box, put both between my lips, and lit them with the Dunhill. With both dangling out of the side of my mouth it was time to test the staff's theory on how strong the bond with Dustin was. *How much did he trust me?*

"Dustin? Hey man, I lit a cigarette for you. If you want it, just hold out your left arm to the side and I'll slide it in between your fingers, then step back to where I am now."

Dustin stretched out his left arm as I started to stand. "I'm getting up. I'm going to walk over and give you this cigarette, no bullshit, okay?"

I got to my feet and glanced back toward the staff. It was like life-sized cardboard cutouts were there instead of the real people, they hadn't moved an inch, still hanging back with the same expressions on their faces, ranging from frightened to panicked. The unknown woman appeared to be biting her nails now. *A terrible habit* I thought before speaking to Dustin's back.

"I'm heading over now, Dustin."

I slowly approached, taking a wider route than I needed to in case he thought I/we were up to something. At the moment, *we* were not. I had left the cigarettes dangling from my lips, and I just realized it. There was enough wind up here to keep the smoke out of my eyes.

"Okay, man here you go."

I slipped the lit cigarette between his first and second fingers on his left hand, then began to slowly walk backward. He never even turned to look at me. "Dustin, I'm going to head back to where I was and sit back down and have this smoke with you," I said much quieter now that I was a couple of feet away from him.

. My heart was ready to burst. The stress of the situation, the nicotine rush from unwittingly taking several drags off the two cigarettes in my mouth, and the proximity to the ledge of this building. I started to do a little side-step, which kept me relatively close to Dustin, but gave me the ability to look from Dustin to the staff, without turning my head too far. My shuffle sideways looked ridiculous and nowhere near natural, but having him, and the staff at 45° seemed like the best move.

I smoked and just looked from Dustin to the staff, not speaking to either. On my third or fourth glance at the staff, all four moved, in unison. Like a starter pistol had gone off—all were starting the hundred-meter-dash, but the judges had called a false start. The race was over, and all the participants knew it. It was slow-motion, like a terrible replay. *Like when Kennedy was shot in the Zapruder film.* As my head swiveled back toward Dustin, one of the staff started to yell.

"Br…"

I heard it, I think. Maybe it was snatched by a gust of

wind before it reached me? Maybe it *did* reach my ear as my head spun, but I refused to let it in.

I saw the last few black hairs on Dustin's head disappear over the edge of that low wall as my eyes regained focus. Before I could move, the staff was rushing to the edge. What they hoped to achieve was beyond my grasp just then.

Two police officers appeared at my side as I attempted to amble up to the ledge, only to have Charles block my way. He knew I didn't need to see Dustin like that. No one needed to see.

I turned and walked away from Charles, sitting back down at the same spot where I had sat and talked to Dustin. I sat down, and I smoked. I glanced up to see Charles only a few feet away, and talking to me. I didn't register a word of it. I would have been completely without feeling if it weren't for the pounding in my head. Charles seemed to talk forever. My god dammed head just wouldn't stop pounding.

Police inquiries, statements given, endless hours of staff meetings, one on one meetings with VPs of this, and VPs of that all took place. Crying, yelling—I resigned from my position at the hospital though I was repeatedly told I was not to blame for what had happened. "Unprecedented," they said. "A terrible series of unfortunate events," they told me. This did nothing to assuage my guilt. I still resigned.

The series of events that led to Dustin being able to access the roof was a woman accidentally leaving a window open, a broken door lock for which no work order could be found, an HVAC contractor who had worked on the rooftop AC unit who simply forgot to let hospital maintenance he was finished, and finally me, who put himself in circumstances above his competency.

During the inquiries, I also found out who the woman on the roof had been. Her name was Mabel Howards-Stein, and she was on the hospital's board of directors. She happened to be in a meeting with Darshan that day when all this went down. I was told by Charles that when she was at Princeton, her friend and roommate had killed herself and she had been racked with guilt over the incident. Though she had never met Dustin, I was told that she took his death hard, and promptly resigned from the board after that day. Dustin's death affected so many people, with many having never met him. Tragedy can create such collateral damage.

After leaving my position at the hospital, I attempted to shift my focus away from helping people. What came with that was isolation from friends and family and many sad nights home alone, and drunk. Dustin's death seemed to give me the excuse to self-destruct. It became easier and easier to shut people out, and I did.

Several years and a career change later, I found myself alone in my apartment, writing and revising my suicide note. I felt broken. On my fifth revision, I put the pen down and called an old friend to ask for help. I needed to do what Dustin could not. My friend stayed on the line with me until another friend, who lived close by, could come and stay with me. I just kept seeing the faces of Charles, Mabel, Darshan, and Sandy as Dustin went over the edge. How can you forget such shock? I became convinced it would haunt me forever.

That day, I was able to pull myself off the ledge and do what Dustin could not. I found a reason to live, even if it was a small one. The light that drove me to help others had gone out, not to be relit. I could no longer help others in need. I had to heal. I still keep others at arm's length but every so often, I let someone in. I am still healing. I'll always be healing.

P.S. A week after Dustin's death, I called the local coroner's office to find out if Dustin's body had been claimed. Sadly, but not surprisingly, it had not. How could I leave him there? Never loved in life and it seemed he could find no dignity in death. I took it upon myself to call a crematorium and have them pick up his body. I was there when he was cremated, and try as I might I couldn't shed a tear.

So, on what should have been Dustin's eighteenth birthday, I scattered his ashes in the ocean off the coast of Galveston, Texas, near docks where all the big cruise ships are moored. I would never know if that memory he had of this place was real, or not.

Rest in peace Dustin.

The Ides of March

I have one older brother, and his birthday is in March, not too far from St. Patrick's Day. With me not knowing a lot about my family history (on either side), this was one of those holidays that typically went unnoticed. Birthday, yes, people drinking green beer, no. Other than the anticipation of the gifts he might receive on his birthday, there would be one additional thing that would give rise to his excitement, a McDonald's Shamrock Shake. He loved it and would try to pack in as many as he could before McDonald's would inevitably remove it from their menu. One of those "For a Limited Time Only" marketing schemes.

Sadly, his fondness for the Shamrock Shake does not persist. It's an unfortunate tale of a childhood ritual cut too short. McDonald's is a formidable foe, and those who dare not respect the arches will pay a heavy price. My brother's love of the Shamrock Shake came to an abrupt and public end inside a busy shopping mall in Toledo, Ohio.

On a Sunday shopping trip to the mall, my mother, my brother, and I picked up lunch at McDonald's. I can remember to this day how busy the mall was. That's probably the kind of thing an introvert remembers, and this trip would have morphed into any other trip to the mall in my memory bank if not for what transpired shortly after lunch. My brother was falling behind, and under constant scrutiny from our mother for it. He was too busy jamming that straw into every corner and nook, slurping up every ounce of that Shamrock Shake. Kids are notoriously bad at doing more than one thing at a time; give them a piece of gum on a walk and they will trip and fall within a few minutes. It wasn't a pretty sight.

When I last looked back at my brother, getting a sense that he was about to have the cup ripped out of his hand and thrown away, he had stopped. Initially, I believed he was distraught over what could be his final Shamrock Shake of the year, but his face wasn't quite telling the same story. *So much drama over a stupid shake,* I was thinking. Any second, he was going to fall to his knees and cry in agony over this green goodness. I was incorrect. My brother suddenly dashed over to the nearest trashcan. Right in the middle of the crowded mall, in front of all the shoppers, he expelled the day's breakfast, lunch, and more importantly, the last Shamrock Shake of his life.

My poor brother was never the same. He was never able to celebrate St. Patrick's Day with a green beer, nor able to stomach a Shamrock Shake again. It was so much worse than the "oh, my, god, I drank too much tequila that time we went to Cancun" anecdote. This episode changed my brother. Green was no longer his second favorite color, he never again wanted to carry cash, his favorite comic—The

Hulk, got thrown in the trash and replaced by The

Fantastic Four, and worst of all, his dream of being a

park ranger when he grew up died that day.

After doing a little research this story, I found

out that the Shamrock Shake is still being sold

around St. Patrick's Day every year at McDonald's.

Hopefully, this hasn't put you off them. Enjoy!

The President on Speed Dial

When I was nineteen or twenty, I worked at a pizza and sub shop. Yes that same pizza and sub shop, but a different pizza and sub shop from that other story. There were two pizza and sub shops. And one pizza shop that I have yet to mention in a story. Yet. Where was I? While we worked, we listened to the radio, a local station that played a cornucopia of modern rock, alternative, and classic rock.

In addition to all the music, the thing I liked about the station was the contests they had. It was a "the eleventh caller will win tickets to the zoo" sort of thing. They would have contests for concert tickets, CDs, gift certificates to local restaurants, and many other giveaways for shit no one needs. It's safe to say that if this particular radio station didn't offer these contests, we may have changed the station early on. I tended to be one of the outspoken few who had difficulty tuning out whatever music was on the radio, so I needed it to be tolerable. I've had this issue my whole life, an inability to tune annoyances out. Even after having a child, I was incapable of tuning out what I found annoying.

The pizza shop had two phones. This was ideal, as when I would hear "the eleventh caller will win…" I would dart to the phone, abandoning my (partially done) pizza/sub and leaving my teammates to finish up my order. They all seemed to find my flamboyant darting around the restaurant entertaining, so I never got any grief for walking away from my food. I was the entertainment for those few seconds it took me to run over to the phone and dial the radio station. Let us be honest, it was not a high-paying job, so no one other than the owners and their family wanted to be there. Also, I ended up winning several contests, so that helped the "fun" factor.

The only limits placed on me were by the radio station itself. The rule was that an individual could only win something once every thirty days. I did not call for every contest, though. Say the radio station was giving out a signed copy of the new Spin Doctors CD, I would skip that one. Even a bored and broke twenty-year-old pizza shop employee understands that there are things in this world that are free for a reason, and a signed copy of a Spin Doctors CD was on that list.

I don't recall all the prizes I won through the radio station over the two years I worked at the pizza/sub shop, but I recollect a few. There was a time when I won front-row tickets to a ZZ Top concert. They were only familiar to me from the videos I saw on MTV and the schtick they had surrounding those crazy long beards. Needless to say, this wasn't my kind of music. I was allowed to put a small sign up near the front register offering up the pair for $50. I then left them in the small safe below and told my coworkers they could have $10 if they sold them, or were responsible for the transaction.

In the end, it only took two days for me to sell them, and luckily, I was on shift so I got the whole $50. My compulsion earned me a few bucks that time around. Another radio contest I won got me two tickets to the Detroit Grand Prix Indycar race. These turned out to not be worth the cost of the paper they were printed on. I *did* go to the race, and after walking around Belle Isle for thirty minutes I was unable to find a suitable enough place to stand that would allow me to see more than the top six inches of the race car as it screamed by at a hundred miles per hour. General admission tickets for a race at a track that is flat and has several feet of barriers and fencing between the track and the spectators, it *was* a bust. I ended up stomping off back to the car, driving home, and watching the remainder on the television.

Most of the other prizes are lost on me because they were just inconsequential junk. For some contests, I would call the radio station and be the third caller, hang up quickly, redial only to be the eighth caller, hang up quickly, then again redial but instead of being the eleventh and winning caller, I'd end up missing it by one and be the twelfth. Fuck, I wanted that new Weezer album.

Other than boredom, I don't know what drove me to repeatedly do this. But as I have mentioned before, I would abandon orders and run off to the phone to call in. This wasn't my first entry into calling strangers for goods and services, or just a nice chat.

When I was twelve, my friends and I were at my home in the summer playing, and the radio happened to be on. There was a call-in show happening, and they dared me to call in and give my opinion. The topic: drinking and driving. This was in the heyday of Mothers Against Drunk Drivers, which was a group that sought to stop drunk driving, help prevent underage drinking, and help those affected by drunk driving. Let's just say when I called in, I took a very libertarian point of view.

Host:

"Caller, you're on the air."

Twelve-year-old me:

"Hi, I just wanted to say what if people want to go out and have a drink or two and then drive home, they should be allowed. What's the big deal?"

Host:

"Thank you for calling in and sharing your opinion with us."

We quickly turned up the radio to hear my last few words, Hard-hitting stuff, I know.

At twelve, I was lucky to even have an opinion on such a grown-up topic, I thought. Oh, who am I kidding, I was just making shit up to be on the radio.

Where could I go from here, I pondered. Could I call a random number in the phone book and tell them their refrigerator was running and they should then go and chase after it? I could call the local bowling alley and ask for Seymour Butts, or a name as equally ridiculous. No, this was mere child's play. I needed to ramp up my game, and who better to call on the phone than the President of the United States? Hey, maybe he'd like to hear my views on drinking and driving.

This was the second term of the Ronald Reagan White House, and you'd think it would be difficult to call the president, but you'd be wrong. The number for the Whitehouse was listed in the phonebook. So, I called.

Whitehouse operator:

"White House, how may I direct your call?"

Me:

"Um, hi. May I please speak with the president?"

White House operator:

"Oh, I'm sorry, he's not available at the moment."

Me:

"Um, okay. Thank you."

White House operator:

"You're welcome, and have a nice day."

This was followed by much giggling and then mild panic that a swarm of government agents would surround my house and take me away for questioning. Of course, none of that happened. These poor operators must have received a hundred dumb calls a day from children who came across the number in the phone book. And we should add in a few lunatics.

This phone obsession wasn't always outgoing, though. A year or two following my failed attempt to reach the president, I started receiving phone calls from a girl I didn't know and who refused to identify herself. She would only tell me we went to school together and that she knew me. I was unfamiliar with her. Intriguing, to say the least. She would call a couple of nights a week and just want to chat with me. Often not knowing anything about her, I didn't have a lot to talk about. She was quite clever and was careful not to give anything away. After a few weeks of this, the farthest I got was that she was in my neighborhood and babysitting a couple of kids. Not very helpful, as there were fifty houses in my neighborhood, and the houses with small children living in them were completely ignored by me. Too loud and too sticky for my liking, so they didn't exist. So, whatever house was hiding this girl, I was to never know.

After a few weeks of chatting, I think she felt the noose was starting to tighten. This game she'd started could not be sustained. I was bound to figure out who she was from her voice, a friend who she'd confided in, or simply me walking around the neighborhood on the nights she babysat and waiting until someone peeped at me through a split in the curtains.

So, with me getting ever closer to finding out her identity she ran for it. She stopped calling me altogether. Shortly after our pleasant phone calls stopped, I had a friend in a class spill the beans, letting me in on the secret. It was *just* a girl who'd been in one of my classes who I didn't know and had never talked to.

I had grown fond of our chats on the telephone and was sad to see them go, and for years after, we never had a conversation. Maybe that period in our lives was awkward for both of us. Or maybe just for me. Other than the phone calls, which again I did enjoy, I wasn't very interested in getting to know her. It was a shame really because when she and I were in high school, we struck up a casual friendship, and I look back on that fondly too. By the time I figured either of us out, I think we were quite similar, and like many middle-school-aged children, I was too concerned with being friends with someone who existed outside of my friendship realm.

Such is life. Such is timing. Often, when you're searching too hard for a friend or a partner, you might latch on to the first one that comes along and forgo the loneliness. Speaking of loneliness, I hope that the couple who purchased those ZZ Top tickets from me had a nice time. The front row at a shitty concert is still the front row.

My Life as a Drag Queen

"Jesus, I thought you were a girl."

This was bellowed in my general direction and often directly in my face more times than I can count when I was young.

"Nope," I'd respond and slink away, not knowing if I should be offended by that or not. It regularly just confused me. I never knew how to feel about being mistaken for a girl. All I could do was smile and try to make the other person feel okay about their mistake. I was an eleven-year-old kid, still far enough away from manhood to know this would be my life for the next couple of years.

I am a slim fella. Throughout my life, I've been called skinny, slim, bones, string-bean, and so on. In the beginning, it was annoying, as if I had a lot of control over it, but as it went on it was just wearing. But I had to be okay with it. What was my alternative?

No one labeled me as effeminate, accused me of being queer, or used the word I would have been called at the time, a fag. I was just seen as a skinny kid, who from behind resembled a young girl. The fact that I had long hair didn't help me, either. My daughter has friends who are boys who have long hair and are much younger than I was when this story is based, and my hope is that aren't bound to some same stereotypes as I was. It feels so much less important today than it did a few decades ago. I hope these boys find a kinder, more understanding world.

What I feel might have been my biggest misstep of all was my missed opportunity as a fabulously, beautiful, outrageously bankable drag queen. I could have been beloved by people, both straight and gay. I would have been the go-to act for the hen night/bachelor/bachelorette parties. My jam would have been: Alanis Morisette's song "Ironic."

Not knowing a lot about this particular world, most of my information has come from the movie, *The Birdcage*. You may call me ignorant, sure. But you could also call me a dreamer.

Five-eleven without heels and well over six-one with them, I would transform into a towering, lovely beast worthy of every stage from Miami to Milan and back to Las Vegas. I could do the heels, maybe with some practice. I could learn to strut, even. I would also need a name for my new, fabulous self. Veronica Stars? Michelle Morisette also has a nice ring. What's a new persona without a great name? A great name that leaves people with no doubt of whom they are referencing. The one, the only, Veronica. Veronica could be the new me.

But, is the mid-forties the new mid-twenties? My new career had succumbed to agism before I could get it off the ground.

A little more research needs to take place before pushing forward.

The questions are:

Q: Would this just be my nighttime gig?

Q: Would my day job need to change?

Q: Do I need to wax everything? How often? Cost?

Q: Will my impeccable grooming be off-putting to my current co-workers?

Q: Does it hurt to pluck your eyebrows?

Q: Is there some contraption that hides your penis?

Q: What color dress looks the best with my hazel eyes?

Q: Could this new life lead to me becoming a stay-at-home wife? Or better yet, trophy wife?

Q: Do I go for sexy underwear or for what's comfortable?

Q: Can I pull off yoga pants?

Q: Should I get a few feminine tattoos?

Q: Are there still those ladies in the mall who help you with makeup?

Answers: None

And finally, is it too much to hope for to think my partner would love me for who I am, both on the stage and off? I can tell you, one thing I am looking forward to is being more comfortable ordering drinks, you know, the ones that have a little umbrella in them. I do love those fruity umbrella-topped cocktails.

So, on my to-do list could be (in no particular order):
Acquire a girlfriend who won't mind holding my hair while I vomit all the night's free drinks back up.
New running shoes: lighter color.
Second gal pal to go with me to try on dresses.
Go back to blonde.
The second hole pierced, buy diamonds.
More time on the rowing machine.
Investigate Taylor Swift and her music. Maybe there's a song I can use.

My queries are endless. Perhaps all the unknowns are what keep me from pursuing this kind of life. One or two things you can work through, but endless questions with no one to seek guidance from are scary.

Beautiful as I might have been back in my day, to now go and don a maxi-length emerald green dress paired with a mid-heel might be too much for me to pull off. I'm just not a spring chicken any longer. My heart aches, like Bette Midler's in *Beaches*, for my youth and beauty.

And if you see me looking at you when you're out on the town, dressed to kill, don't worry I'm not checking you out. I'm just thinking: I'd look better in that than you do.

No Thanks, I'll Walk

I'm embarrassed to say this, but I have a fear of public transportation, especially buses. I once jumped on a bus in Dublin, Ireland, and while the patrons on board were extremely nice and helpful, they didn't understand where I was saying I wanted to go. Do I even need to mention that virtually everyone in Ireland speaks English?

"We are trying to get to the ga-ol" I said.

"To, the, ga-ol?" they would repeat back to me. Sweat began to form on my brow.

"Sorry," I went on embarrassingly "No. To the ja-ol?" I tried a slightly different pronunciation and slowed my speech. I was getting nowhere.

"Do you have a map?" the kind person who was leading this inquiry asked.

I pulled out the map and pointed down to the place we were going, or hoping to go.

"See, G-A-O-L" I spelled out as a kindergarten teacher would.

"Ahhhhh." Apprehension now dawned on those surrounding us. "Jail?" Someone said sheepishly.

"Jail?" I repeated bewildered.

"Yes, the jail. That's where you are wanting to go?" The folks around us were even embarrassed at this point. They turned to the driver and told him what stop we needed, and he told us the fee. We paid and sat down.

"We'll let you know when your stop is coming up," one of the women from the group said as we walked away and looked for seats.

"Thanks," I said to everyone and my feet.

Fucking jail, I thought. The place was called Kilmainham Gaol. I knew it was a prison and should have been able to comprehend the pronunciation. The gaol, or jail was now just a museum not having housed a prisoner since the mid-1920s. Kilmainham was well known because it was where the leaders of the 1916 Easter Rising insurrection had been not only housed, but also executed. Simply put, the insurrection sought to gain Irish independence from British rule. The leaders are now seen by many as heroes. They were executed at the prison less than a month after the 1916 Rising. One of the leaders, James Connolly was unable to stand because of wounds he received during the fighting, so he was shot by firing squad while seated.

After paying our few-Euro fee and finding seats, we were treated like children who needed looking after. This obviously would not give them a very good impression of Americans, though given I seemed so clueless and my girlfriend at the time never even spoke a word, they could have deduced we had special needs.

The kind people of Dublin took great care to let us know when the stop was coming up and when we walked to get off, we were given *very* specific instructions to where the entrance of Kilmainham

Gaol was located. They understood I was an idiot, with a mute in tow. We found the entrance to Kilmainham Gaol and when finished with the tour walked back to our hotel in the city. *Buses*, I thought *who needs 'em*?

As if another example of my transportation idiocy needs to be brought up, I just can't seem to help myself. I was living in Boulder, Colorado and my car had broken down. Broken down might be an overstatement. It turned out a battery cable had come loose, so when I went to start my car, nothing. Again, I am hesitant to use the term "broken down" because if I had found the battery, I could have easily fixed it.

Listen, I *did* look for it, I just couldn't find it. One could have argued that the size of the car should guarantee success in finding the battery, no? Well, it was an old VW Beetle, which hardly had room for four children inside, had a hamster on a wheel instead of an engine, and what people these days call a "frunk" housed the gas tank. I shouldn't even bring up that when I hit a bump, it shuttered, bucked, and jumped into oncoming traffic as if it were determined to kill me.

The battery, as it turned out, was under the back seat. Who knew! I called my father back in Michigan, and as he explained the location of the battery, he spoke very slowly and deliberately because he understood as all others already know, that I was an idiot. While on the phone making an ass out of myself, I decided to inquire about the heat and how the hell that shit even worked. *If* it existed at all.

"There are two levers between the seats right next to where you insert your seatbelt that controls the heat. They should be labeled," my dad said patiently.

"That's what those levers do?" I said, laughing in amazement. "All the words are rubbed off, so I wasn't sure what those did. They look like levers that will eject the seats." I felt a little less blameless now that I knew the words explaining what they did had been rubbed off, possibly since the 1970s. There was no Google when this took place, so the only searchable index I could utilize was my father's brain.

But on that day my car didn't start, I needed to get to work. So, I panicked. I didn't think to make a quick call to my father, as I assumed this was some larger issue and I didn't have time to troubleshoot it with him. I had to get going, but how? My roommate had already left for work, so he was out. Anyone else I might have known, either I assumed was unavailable or my embarrassment kept me from calling and asking for a favor. There *was* a bus stop though, just up the road from our apartment but not having any idea how public transportation in the area worked, I just froze.

The incident in Dublin was years off, but I was already scared of public transportation. I don't believe it is agoraphobia, which is a fear of public transportation, or even trochophobia, which is a fear of trucks and buses. I mostly have a phobia of feeling like an idiot, which I don't believe is a diagnosable phobia. I didn't understand how it all worked, and I couldn't bring myself to go over to the bus stop and just figure it out. The payment method perplexed me as well. *How the hell do you pay for it?* I pondered. I was usually flat broke at this time in my life, so I might not have had the cash to pay the fare.

There were routes to worry about along with the payment. What if I got on one going the wrong way? I could conceivably spend my cash on a bus trip in the wrong direction. I was panicking, but not for long. I needed to get to work, so that was exactly what I did. And how did I do that? I walked.

I threw my work clothes on and began my six-plus-mile journey to the office supply store where I worked. I was also new to the city of Boulder, so I would need to take the same route I would have driven. This had me running across divided highways, frantically scampering through busy intersections, and finally onto pedestrian sidewalks.

Once I arrived my colleagues were baffled by my appearance *and* my nearly two-hour tardiness. I let them know I had car trouble and had to walk "the rest of the way" and to not worry, I was okay. This was not a great situation I'd landed myself in. It took me well over two damn hours to walk to work that morning, and if I couldn't get over my pride, I would be facing a two-hour walk home.

On the walk, I'd had a lot of time to imagine how one could successfully ride the city bus, but I had no more practical knowledge than I had earlier that morning before setting out. So, rather than asking a coworker for a ride back to my apartment, I did the only thing I could think of to do when my shift ended: I walked. I would do the journey again, in reverse.

Ignorance can come in so many varieties. Because I was so ignorant of how the public transportation system worked in my area, I spent over four hours walking to and from my apartment that day. Being ignorant, you might not see a way out, or you might choose to ignore all rational thought and try to resolve an issue like this by yourself. I just kept telling myself I would call my father when I got home and he would help me.

Now in my late forties, I've been able to navigate the subway in New York City, the London Underground, and various other city public transportation methods without any problem. As for buses, nope. The embarrassment in Dublin kept me off all buses for almost two decades. I've considered always keeping a twenty-dollar bill in my wallet just in case I need to catch one. In today's world of cars on-demand, I might be off the hook. In most places, I travel, there will be an Uber or Lyft available, a few clicks away. The days of the city bus needn't be a burden to me, anymore. Technology has allowed me to sidestep my fear.

Traveling for work over the past several years has also allowed me to navigate the largest airports, be it JFK in New York, Hartsfield-Jackson in Georgia, or London Heathrow abroad. None of that intimidates me. They are all the same basic design once you get inside them. If an internal train or tram isn't available, there should be a shuttle bus around. There's usually plenty of signage available to the weary traveler if they are just able to look up.

None of this traveling comes without its pains, though. On a recent trip back from Portland, Oregon, to see a friend, I arrived at my home airport in Detroit to find my luggage didn't come out of the chute onto the carousel. I stood there until all my fellow passengers had retrieved their bags, hands on my hips, annoyed. Customer Service was a short walk, and I was first in line to inquire about my luggage. I let the woman at the counter know my last name and my flight number, and she mashed the keys, obviously not wanting to put up with my troublesome face.

"It's on eight," she said, looking up after speaking.

"Eight? The board says twelve, and everyone else on my flight already got their luggage off the carousel," I pleaded.

"It's on eight," she repeated. "Did you check it?"

She looked at me as if I was the cause of her current lot in life. Suppose she didn't get a lot of happy customers coming into her area, so maybe I *was* part of the problem.

I glanced over my shoulder, and I could just make out the number eight in the distance. It was dark and I also didn't see anyone near the thing.

"No," I exclaimed. "It looks dark, I'm guessing…"

"Well, it should be there," she said cutting me off.

I let out a sigh and left the area, walking toward carousel eight. And wouldn't you know it, there it was. Sitting, alone. There was no one else around, and it appeared to have been there for some time.

"Fuckers," I said out loud as I approached the bag.

After getting the bag home, I opened it and discovered a TSA paper inside stating that the bag had been searched. *No shit*, I thought. The bag had skipped my layover in Minneapolis/St. Paul and gone right on through to Detroit, without me.

I had no reservations about going into Customer Service and asking about my bag or navigating my way through airports domestic and foreign, but buses are still elusive. Hell, maybe I do have a phobia.

After completing my (shortened) shift at the office supply store in Boulder, I set off for home. Another six miles lay ahead. I did it once; I could do it, again. As I walked out the doors, I was feeling embarrassed that I couldn't ask any of my coworkers for a ride, even though I did have a casual friendship with many of them. I walked on and grumbled about how I'd let myself down, how I should be more forthcoming, outgoing, and brave, and how tired I'd started to feel.

The next thing I knew a Volkswagen Fox pulled into a driveway in front of me, and the passenger window was rolled awkwardly down to reveal a smiling driver I recognized.

"Hey!" he yelled across the passenger seat and out the open window.

It was Ken, a guy I had worked with at a previous job and stayed in touch with.

"What are you doing, walking home?" he said, laughing. "I knew it was you, that bouncy walk you have."

"My car is broken," I said, now slouching to peer into the passenger window.

"Get in man, I'll give you a ride."

Ken gave me a ride back to my apartment. I was so thankful, but I hardly had enough gas to put in my VW Beetle, so I didn't have any to spare to show him how thankful I was. He was a good friend while I lived there. I was home alone on Christmas day one year, and he was kind enough to swing by and drop off some food on his way to a Christmas party. That was one of the kindest things I've ever had someone do for me.

After Ken left that day, I called my father, and this was when we had a conversation about the battery location on the Beetle. I was again grateful that he attempted to soften the blow by telling me the battery cables could easily come undone, creating a situation the same as I found myself in that day.

My dad was spot on—it was the battery cable. It had come loose, rendering my car inoperable. I would be saved from walking or trying to figure out Boulder's public transportation system for one more day. At the end of the day, I had walked no less than seven miles, pissed off my manager, proven to my father I had no idea how a car worked, inconvenienced Ken, and demonstrated to myself that I was socially awkward to the point of pain and probably death.

Now, back to this bouncy walk business. This has been an annoyance of mine my whole life. I've spent hours walking around my various houses, apartments, etc. trying to remedy or lessen the amount of bounce in my walk. This flummoxed me until well into my forties, when I was watching this British chat show. An English actor was being interviewed, and he had mentioned his bouncy walk and that he had a film director assign him some help in correcting it. What he went on to say was so simple and yet so profound. The helper had told this actor to think heel-toe, heel-toe as he walked. That was it, the simple solution I had always needed. I tried it, and like magic, my bouncy walk diminished. The hardest part is doing it consistently. Now, it's chewing gum while walking and talking to yourself constantly: heel-toe, heel-toe.

So, just like getting the Beetle going again, my bouncy walk turned out to be an easy fix. My fear of busses, not so easy.

Photography as a Service

In 2009, a week after my thirty-fifth birthday, I started a photography business. I was always the guy with the good gear, who while being strictly a hobbyist photographer, received compliments on my photos, even having several national papers post a picture I had taken of a post-Hurricane Katrina-ravaged Biloxi, Mississippi shortly after the storm.

By the time I hit my mid-thirties, I was ready for a change. I had burned myself out, trying to work through the social work field, so I felt a natural progression was to pick a profession that would pay as poorly as social work but without human interaction. I also had enough relationship baggage to fill an airport carousel, and the number of them who would gladly see me thrown off the top of the

Burj Khalifa building should bring me to dig a moat around my home and fill it with alligators. I needed to keep my distance from people for a while. Maybe for good.

I joined any and every photography group I could find, in the real world and online. I floated my name and business around the county where I lived. I signed up for a couple of photography classes at two local universities, which I would later explain to the IRS were business expenses.

Being a full-time photographer, especially one who deals mainly with landscapes can be challenging. So, with mediocre prospects on the horizon and the thought of buying more Ramen noodles by the case, I decided to take radical action. After dipping into my dwindling savings, I acquired a couple of Nikon SB-600 professional flashes to go with my Nikon D3S, with which I ended up booking a couple of shooting gigs for the coming fall. Weddings. The exact thing I was trying to avoid. I was learning that being a full-time photographer was tough, but I was determined to stick with it, even if I had to deal with a few brides and grooms now and then.

It is not difficult to do the work if you can stomach being overly nice and obedient for a day. What I didn't anticipate was that all this human interaction would take me back to my social work days and dealing with patients. In between two separate photography jobs taken that fall, I could be found bent over the hood of my car, eyes screwed shut in a full-blown panic attack. If I wanted to get back to landscapes and travel photography, I had to stick to these weddings, despite the fact they caused me internal discomfort.

Early the following year, I was hired to shoot a winter wedding on Mackinac Island, which is a beautiful spot located just north of the very top of the lower peninsula of Michigan. It was a referral from one of my previous weddings—family friends. Referrals are the bread and butter of the wedding photography business. Do a good job shooting a dozen weddings, and the referrals from those could keep you going for a while, maybe even years depending on your clientele.

The late January wedding on Mackinac Island was for a couple I'll call the Fullers. The bride and groom Fuller were an attractive young couple, and the backdrop of the island in winter made it such an easy shoot that it would have been hard to mess it up. Good-looking people don't require tricky angles and creative lighting, they're just attractive. I had no way of knowing then that shooting this wedding would have such an impact on my life.

The bride Fuller came from old Michigan manufacturing money. The kind of money where the bride doesn't need to discuss with her fiancé why her new last name will be hyphenated, and why he's signing paperwork drawn up by lawyers before the big day about what will happen to him if he strays, and another dozen ways on how he will be left penniless upon marital dissolution. Some of this was merely conjectured on my part, though after a couple of drinks, many of the groomsmen and bridesmaids tend to get, um, chatty.

It all went smoothly. Bride hyphenated-Fuller and groom Fuller were cordial and kind, and the shoot and picture printing and delivery went well. All my printing was farmed out to an old friend, Jason. He had been a software developer at Adobe responsible for early versions of what would later become a program called Lightroom. Jason, a workaholic, and man of little materialistic wants, did this work for basically free. Jason was always up for a new challenge, and he had only one rule, no information about the couple was to be shared. Jason wanted them to remain anonymous. He would see them no differently than a one-hour photo employee. The photos were there to process, their taker, their stories, superfluous information.

I was given a free room as there was no boat off the island in the evenings during wintertime so after a long day of shooting, I quickly scanned over the photos for issues, then turned in and slept for twelve hours. I packed the next morning, took a boat back to the mainland, and other than picture processing and cashing their check, I put the Fuller job behind me.

Fast-forward four rather quiet months, work-wise. I had traveled out west to Arches National Park to shoot some climbers. I was doing my best to get my foot in the door of the travel photography/outdoor lifestyle world. The scenery was stunning, and I was able to hook up with a couple of climbers via email beforehand who were interested in being shot. At the very least, I could get a few good photos for my portfolio. I did it all on the cheap, taking a Greyhound bus out to Utah, all the while clutching my camera gear to my chest like a newborn baby.

After returning from Utah, I was going through my work email and came across what I believed to be a legitimate job offer: a referral originating from the Fuller job, the friends of theirs who said I was coming highly recommended. This wasn't a wedding shoot, though, since the couple was already married. Instead, the husband (who was the primary emailer) asked if I was interested in taking them on as clients. The husband used the word "lifestyle" and "natural" during our email exchanges. Red flags?

A few emails in, and still not understanding what was being asked of me, I decided to throw out an hourly rate so high no reasonable person would find it acceptable. Without hesitation, the husband agreed to my preposterous rate, along with a two-hour minimum. I typed up a pre-paid contract and sent it over immediately. The only details I was given were to meet them at a park and we'd do a stroll-and-shoot. The only reason I could come up with for the shoot was for social media posts and perhaps a framed photo or two for their home. We'll call this couple the Colliers.

The Colliers were an attractive couple, roughly the same age as I was at the time. They showed up smartly dressed, but since I am usually preoccupied with lighting, backdrop, and angles, I don't tend to notice what couples are wearing. One thing that did stand out to me was Mr. Collier's watch. Or should I say, both their watches? I know enough about watches that I could recognize that both Colliers had Patek Philippe brand watches, and just one of them could have been sold to buy a very nice condo in my city—together, they could buy a small home in Savannah, Georgia.

The Colliers were nothing but professional, courteous, and a little assertive. The park shoot was finished in a little over two hours, and I would easily clear a grand for the job. Jason did the digital touch-up and sorted through the photos for me; I sent the final photos via a download link to Mr. Collier so he could access all the files at his convenience. I paid a few bills, which wiped out that grand I cleared, but after that, I'd put the job behind me, or so I thought.

A week later, I received an email from Mrs. Collier. My first thought was mild panic, that there was an issue with one or several of the photos I'd taken. It was also strange receiving an email from Mrs. Collier because I had only corresponded with her husband on the previous job. The email was to inquire about a meeting. She wanted to discuss a new project she and her husband had been working on. It was one of those "details to follow" kind of things. She let me know we'd discuss some of the details in the meeting, which she set for 6 p.m. four days from the day I read it, and I would be paid for my time. Curious, and in need of money, I emailed her back, accepting the meeting.

This felt like a mansion shoot from the off, so I did my best to put it out of my mind for the next couple of days. Was I here to take pictures to sell the place? It made me uneasy. I never liked working in the vague, so every time it crept in, I felt a little uneasy. This was a couple who had overpaid for a simple walkabout shoot, and now I was beginning to wonder if that had been a test. It's always best not to dwell on the unknown. If I was moving toward something immoral, or just plain strange, I would be finding out in a few days.

I arrived at their home promptly at six. Their house sat near the edge of town, where land and privacy could be acquired. It was the kind of sprawling neighborhood that wasn't inviting. A place that wouldn't see trick-or-treaters on Halloween. The power and the money that comes with such places are too intimidating for all outsiders. This didn't appear to be new construction. If you have enough money, even the new can be made to look old.

The Colliers met me at the door upon my arrival and welcomed me in. They led the way to a sitting room, which had a country-modern kind of vibe. The wagon-wheel chandelier dangling from the ceiling was affixed to heavy iron chains and held actual candles; the whole thing looked 1850s authentic, or maybe I was being fooled by a television prop. This chandelier could have hung in the Long Branch Saloon on the set of *Gunsmoke* for the duration of its run. Wealthy people understand that when a unique piece is on display guests will ask about it. Authenticity can lend itself to interesting chatter, but probably not as much as an authentic piece of Hollywood memorabilia. I sort of expected to see a taxidermied bear standing erect in the corner. Thankfully, the Colliers spared me that mild moment of panic.

"Children?" I asked as an icebreaker as we walked into the room.

"Nope," swiftly came from the husband.

"Neither of us ever wanted any," Mrs. Collier chimed in. "And it seems better to regret not having them than regret having them."

"Please, have a seat." Mr. Collier gestured toward a brown leather couch on our right, directly across from an identical couch separated by a coffee table made from a tree stump a foot thick and three feet in diameter.

"Very cool," I said, looking down at the coffee table before sitting on the couch.

"Thanks," Mr. Collier replied, letting out a little groan as he and his wife sat down.

I waited for a story, but none came. "We opened a Cab, and sorry to say we started without you," the wife said with a smile.

There was a third empty glass placed in front of where I was now sitting. Mrs. Collier leaned over, and as she began to tip the bottle toward my glass, she blurted out.

"Oh sorry, I didn't ask you if you wanted any." Now she was chuckling at her joke.

"I'll take half a glass, sure," I said with a grin.

Red wine isn't my thing, but I certainly didn't want to seem rude. I was once told by a boss of mine that he never trusted someone who doesn't drink alcohol. While on its face that's a completely ridiculous statement, I've always remembered there *are* people in this world who think this way. One of my primary goals as a photographer was that I remained neutral. I was that house that goes up for sale, stripped of all personal effects. If I cannot learn this skill, I will starve.

All three wine glasses dealt with, Mrs. Collier handed her husband his, grabbed her own, and slid back onto the couch.

"Sorry for all the cloak and dagger," her husband started. "I thought we could share a little something with you about the job. Without giving *too* much away."

His tone was light, but not overly playful. A man who had business to discuss. A man who was used to seriously discussing all business, whether warranted or not.

"We would like to hire you for another job," Mr. Collier began slowly. He almost looked a little apprehensive now.

"This one is a little more sensitive in nature."

Here was the payoff. Why I was brought out to this home? What depravity lay ahead?

"Oh?" I said, eyebrows raised.

"There is nothing illegal about what we're asking, I assure you," Mrs. Collier said confidently.

She was sipping the last of her wine and now wore a grin. I couldn't comprehend its nature, or its meaning. For all I knew, I could soon be overtaken by large men in black suits charging in from an adjacent room, only to be dismembered in a bathtub and used as an ingredient in a stew.

Mrs. Collier sat forward, still grinning. "Yes. So, we spend time with a group of people."

Shit, sex stuff.

The husband then joined his wife near the edge of the couch.

"What she is trying to say is we're part of a group of people who have a particular type of party."

Double-shit, swingers. Don't panic.

"I can see your wheels turning," Mrs. Collier said gesturing toward my head. "It's *not* exactly what you're thinking."

"Are you sure?" I asked with a wry little smile on my face.

I set my empty wine glass on the stump. Mr. Collier leaned forward without saying a word and refilled all the wine glasses, emptying the bottle, even though I didn't ask for more. There was undoubtedly more coming my way to digest. "What we need is a discreet photographer. To take pictures at an *adult* party. Discretion." She emphasized that last word. "We need you for a few late-night hours on a to-be-named Saturday evening, leading into Sunday morning. Three hours—if we go over, you'll be paid half again as much. Discretion." She again emphasized that last word.

We sat in silence as they studied my expression. I had learned through years of social work to bury your feelings and personal details from patients. Blank slate. Use expressions only for the patient to reflect off. Remember the house for sale, stripped of all personal detail, appealing to *any* buyer.

"What do you think?" Mr. Collier said in the calmest demeanor I'd seen yet. The wine must have been kicking in.

Fucking red wine.

I hesitated. I wanted to make sure the Colliers understood I had given this enough thought. That I recognized I now held the power in the conversation. That my answer was my final answer. Once my answer was given this conversation would be over, and I would be out the door within just a couple of minutes.

"You can pay me for six, and I'll shoot for two. I can write up a confidentiality agreement if you'd like, and you can have every picture, including the memory cards, when I am finished. I will also come alone, without an assistant."

The Colliers appeared to be unfazed by any of my ultimatums. It can be difficult to amass a fortune without understanding who you're doing business with. The Colliers had likely done their research on me. Perhaps the knew the status of my bank accounts, my debts, my failed relationships, and the abrupt end to my career as a social worker. Social work was a poor man's profession to the Colliers. They heard the word "social worker" and it only conjured up images of children left at fire stations, homeless drug addicts, perpetual welfare moms, and a squandered education.

"We need a camera set up on a tripod with a remote-control shutter release. A welcome station for our guests, and we can have someone operate that until you arrive. After you arrive, I need you to mingle with the guests. There are no restrictions on what, or whom, you can take pictures of."

The husband looked over at his wife for confirmation, which he received.

"Let's call it three hours for five thousand. If you're not in your car and driving away within fifteen minutes after those three hours, I'll give you another thousand. I'll throw in another five hundred for the memory cards. I want you to shoot—a lot."

I drained the rest of my wine, which gave me time to respond. I let out a small sigh before I could stop myself, an old habit that I just couldn't kick.

"What's the date?" I say looking to the husband, then wife, then back to the husband.

"The twenty-first. Saturday after next" Mrs. Collier told me.

"If you want this welcome station set up beforehand, that's thirty minutes that will eat into the three hours. Agreed?"

"Agreed," Mrs. Collier said nodding. "Station setup should be at eight, then we'll need you back at eleven. Thirty minutes for the station, another two and a half hours shooting the party, correct?"

"Correct," I said in agreement.

Husband and wife looked at each other in silent acknowledgment then turned back to me.

"See you on the twenty-first at 8 p.m. then," I said getting up.

"I'll walk you out," Mr. Collier said standing up.

Shit, what did I just agree to?

This played over and over in my head. I'd walked right into it and given them exactly what they wanted. I was never in control of that situation.

The god damn rich.

I glanced back over my shoulder at the house and Mr. Collier standing in the doorway, undoubtedly judging my Jeep.

"Email me anything else I might need to know. I'll get the contract sent over tomorrow."

"Sure thing," Mr. Collier said somewhat cheerfully.

As promised, the following day I sent a contract over to Mr. Collier. Then, over the proceeding four-to-five days, Mr. Collier and I hashed out the rest of the details, with the initial financial and time agreement still in place. My shooting time would be from 11 p.m. until 1:30 a.m. I would set up the stationary welcome station with a remote shutter at 8 p.m. This would be in the first room on the right off the entryway and would be cleared of all furniture before my arrival. I would have thirty minutes to set up, test, and confirm it was working. Thirty minutes seemed like an acceptable amount of time for this, but it's always the unknowns that catch you out.

I should have billed like a lawyer for all the back and forth. I would have to investigate my pricing model after this shoot. All the details were set for the twenty-first, and I still felt uneasy about it. I decided to confide in a couple of close friends about it. *If* the whole thing did go sideways, I had enough details to share, an address, date, time, and last name felt like enough. I wanted someone to know what would be on that evening in case something happened. My dear friend and photo helper Jason let me know he'd set an alarm and would expect a text or a call by 1:45 a.m. on the twenty-second. "No word by 2 a.m. and I'm going over there and banging on their fucking door, man," he told me as we sat in his home office, going over the few details I had.

Jason had always had a little flair for the dramatic. I knew he rarely was asleep before bar closing time, but I appreciated the gesture. I wrote all the info down for him, and he pinned it to the large whiteboard on his office wall. Again, always the dramatic, he grabbed a red dry-erase marker and circled it six or seven times, giving it prominence on the board over his other project notes.

The days leading up to the Collier shoot were spent checking equipment, going outdoors, shooting around town, and then rechecking equipment. I made a couple of visits to my local camera shop to buy appropriate memory cards. One I had to return because it was defective. That also made me inquire from whom the camera shop purchased *their* cards. The answer I got back was what I wanted to hear—from the manufacturer. While it's great to save a few bucks on things like memory cards when buying from that big online reseller, the authenticity of the items is often in question, at least by me. In my short time as a professional photographer and interfacing with the same, I'd heard countless stories of issues stemming from counterfeit memory cards and even counterfeit camera lenses. Even if I had to hand these over to the Colliers before walking out the door, I needed reliable equipment, as well as reliable backups for my primary gear. And don't even get me started on backups—pain in the ass.

The twenty-first quickly arrived. I pulled up to the Colliers' home, and it looked no different than my last visit. You couldn't ascertain *anything* was happening here this evening. I don't know what I expected, but I felt prepared for anything. Camera bag with my identical Nikon D3S's inside, tripod in hand, I approached the front door. This was good money for a night's work.

After a few knocks, Mrs. Collier answered the door. Upon the door opening, my gaze floated past her and whatever words were coming out of her. Not until she stepped aside and beckoned me in did, I register what she was saying. The home looked no different, and as I followed Mrs. Collier to the room I'd be setting up in, she looked a bit too casual to be soon hosting a party. When we reached the room a couple of seconds later, I found it empty, just as the Colliers had told me it would be. The door sat in the middle of the wall, so I hesitated for a second, waiting for guidance.

"You can set your equipment up here, I think?" Mrs. Collier gestured to the wall opposite the doorway.

"That will work," I said, walking in and pulling my camera bag off my shoulder, setting it on the mahogany wood floor, then putting the tripod in what I roughly believed to be the right spot. "And how many people will be standing there at a time?"

"Two," Mrs. Collier answered without hesitation.

"I think your husband said you'd be providing a backdrop for the guests to stand in front of?"

"Exactly."

"I have the perfect lens for that," I said, reaching into my bag and pulling out one of the D3S's and my 85mm lens. "After I get this seated on my tripod, I'll need to take a couple of test shots to make sure the lighting and position are where they need to be. Can you stand where you think your guests will stand? I also brought some painter's tape to mark the floor. You can either leave it for the night or take it up."

"Okay," my willing participant replied.

After affixing the lens, I powered the camera up and seated it on the tripod. I spent the next couple of minutes adjusting the positioning as Mrs. Collier fiddled with the lights.

"Okay, if I can have you stand here," I gestured to where I believed the couples would be.

Mrs. Collier was an obedient helper for the few minutes it took to get the positioning correct. I marked off two spots on the floor where her guests should stand, took a few pics, showed them to her, then hooked up the remote shutter and gave her a lesson. A couple more test pics with both of us standing on the tape just to be sure, and then we were done. I picked up the camera bag off the floor and checked my watch: 8:23.

"Thanks for your help," I said as Mrs. Collier led me back toward the front door.

"See you at eleven," she said, opening the door to let me out.

I nodded in agreement as I walked out. "Eleven. See you then."

Time to wait. I grabbed a burger on the way home and then popped in the DVD of Wall-E, which I was pretty sure has been sitting unopened next to my TV since it showed up from Netflix two weeks earlier. *I should cancel that service.* As the movie played, I checked and rechecked my camera, the lenses, battery levels, and the memory cards I'd be leaving at the Colliers' tonight. A shame to lose these new 1TB cards, but oh well. I couldn't finish Wall-E but what I saw of it I liked. *Guess if I make it through tonight, I'll watch the rest tomorrow.*

Rolling up to the Colliers was unnerving. It was dark, *really dark.* So dark that I was afraid I was at the wrong house. As I crept up the driveway a single light came near the front stoop. I drew closer and realized it was a person with a small flashlight. This was the only clue anything was happening at this house tonight. And where the hell was the cars? Did the Colliers have enough clout in the community to have the street lights powered off?

The mysterious person with the flashlight left the porch and walked into the middle of the half-moon-shaped driveway, awaiting my arrival, all the while making small circles with the flashlight in his hand. I stopped the car a few feet in front of him and he switched off the flashlight. Jesus, these people were going to some lengths.

"Evening, sir" the man communicated softly after opening my driver's-side door.

"Evening," I groaned after leaning over and grabbing my camera bag from the passenger seat of my Jeep.

I exited my vehicle, and the man handed me a small coin.

"For your car, sir."

I turned the coin over in my hand, only lit by the Jeep's dome light. *A bit elaborate,* I thought.

"Please go on in, sir. No need to knock."

The man then entered my vehicle and sat looking straight ahead, as if I didn't exist. After crossing over the front of the vehicle, I heard it roll slowly away, headlights still off. Was this something that was practiced ahead of time? What a peculiar situation I'd found myself in. I then did what I was told and walked into the house, glancing down at my watch just before opening the door. Right on time, 11 p.m. I opened the door and was greeted by another man, slightly older than me in age and prematurely graying.

"You are right on time, sir."

This guy was a pro, you could see it. A former maître d' for a high-end restaurant for sure. Here was a man who would speak only when spoken to. A service business veteran, who took his talk so seriously that he might not even give up under torture.

"Your equipment is ready to be collected, sir."

He led me over to the room I had set up the tripod, and there it still sat, with my Nikon D3S on top. There was no backdrop against the opposite wall. Everything had been cleared away. This level of detail frightened me.

"May I collect the memory card, sir?"

"Yeah, give me just a sec."

I unscrewed the mount and ejected the card. I had put a different color dot on each of the cards: red, blue, and green. The blue dot was still on the card I pulled from the camera. I handed it to the maître d', pulled the 1TB card with a green dot out of my pocket, inserted it into the Nikon, and stuffed the camera into my bag. Not one to leave a mess, I walked around the maître d', then pulled the painter's tape off the floor.

"Okay, we can go," I said, rolling up the tape into a ball, stuffing it into my bag, and pulling it up by the handle.

"Follow me, sir."

My heart had not pounded this hard since the fall and my panic attack. I pondered where I was going, and why were there *no* people around? I strained to hear the conversation, music, anything. This *was* a party, right?

A few short steps and I was farther into the house than I had ever been. A dimly lit hallway, a formal dining room, consisting of a table and maybe twelve chairs. We turned a corner, and the world began to brighten. A distant *something* could have been heard. It was faint. Nothing I could make out. I'd have said techno or house music, but that could be my mind playing tricks on me, since I seemed to expect it. Or maybe it was the pounding of my heart.

We reached double frosted doors. The maître d' slid them aside, and as my heart skipped a beat, assuming this was the great reveal, beyond were only two stairways, one up and one down. Taking the down staircase, which spiraled to the right as it descended, led us to another door, frosted glass only on the top half this time. I could see light, movement, and the growing bass I had felt as we descended the staircase that led us here, to its climax, here beyond this door. We had not spoken since walking out of that first room.

If the maître d' let out a sigh before opening the door, I couldn't have heard it over the noise. He did hold, just for a second, before opening it though. Dramatic effect—nice touch. I reached down into my bag to grab one of my Nikon cameras.

When he opened the door, he revealed the secrets of the world. The secrets of the very rich. And what greeted me?
Clowns.

Clowns drinking, clowns fucking, clowns smoking, clowns dancing. Clowns, clowns, and more clowns. It was a god-damned nightmare.

With my finger poised on the shutter button, I stepped through the doors and went to work.

Into my nightmare, and yours.

Rock On

I wanted to contribute something beautiful to the world. A small twitch upward at the corner of the mouth was all I was going for. Not even a full smile, just a smirk would do.

An all-out assault on my daughter's elementary school, by painted rocks.

I tend to do so little for others. I'm happy to cut a check for a cause, be it for animals, racial injustice, flowers for an overworked staff, or a Target gift card for a teacher. But these things take up so little of my time. I did spend a few years doing actual volunteer work for animal shelters, even being interviewed for a local paper for my dedication to a specific cat shelter that was a two-hour drive from my home at the time. It was good press for a place I loved to go, and it took my mind off any troubles that lay outside—a form of therapy for me. While I tend to think I'm a selfish bastard and will gladly inform new and old friends of this very important piece of information on an annual basis, it might just be my posturing. When I race offroad on my motorbike and come across a stranded rider, I always come to a screeching halt beside them and bellow over through my helmet and over the noise of my bike "Hey, you okay?"

After receiving a response, I blast off again. I have tried to look upon this as some form of Karma, wherein me asking others if they need assistance will come back to me in kind. Though I tend to crash every race, they are often very minor and typically don't require assistance from others.

At a race in Nevada, I was fighting with sand and ruts when the bike started to slip away from me. After careening off track I bounced off a cactus (or two), and when I regained my composure, I stopped to assess the damage. I had several spines/glochids sticking out of my left pantleg and in my left arm. Up until that point, I had only raced in either Michigan, Indiana, or Ohio. Riding in these states, when I ventured off the sandy, rocky, muddy track. I would just end up in the woods. This could cause a few issues, but as long as you could avoid running headlong into a tree, you'd probably be alright. As I looked down at the spines sticking out of my leg, I realized they had gone into my knee braces and the thick of my pants.

"Nice," I said acrimoniously, examining it.

The next thing out of my mouth was "uh oh" after I looked at my left arm and saw several spines that had gone through my jersey and into my forearm. As I sat on my bike wondering what to do about this, a rider screamed up to me, stopped, and jumped off his bike.

"I got you, man," he said with haste.

As he came around my side, he already had his backpack off and was unzipping it and reaching inside.

"You okay? I saw you bounce off that cactus," he said as he got to my left side, multitool in hand. He stopped to assess my left half.

"Damn," he said, a little too solemnly for my liking.

"The ones in my leg are in my knee brace, so I can't feel them," I responded. I then held up my left forearm to show him. "These got me though."

He seemed unsure of what to do for a second. Then he snapped out of it and said, "I need to take those out. It's going to hurt."

I was pumping adrenaline, hard. The race, the near-crash, and now the cactus spines protruding from me.

"It's cool, pull them out," I said with more urgency than I should have. "Then I'll get going."

"Okay, hold out your arm," he responded.

He used the plier end of the multitool and pulled them all out. I remember him wincing as he pulled the larger ones: probably two or three inches out of my arm. The pain was pretty minor. My mind had already moved on, back to the race and what other terrors lay ahead.

"Alright man, you good?" he asked after finishing.

"Yeah, thanks man I appreciate it." I laughed a little at the ridiculous situation I'd found myself in.

"Be safe," he told me as I fired up my bike and he disappeared behind me.

"Thanks!" I shouted out as I headed off.

Truth be told the guy who stopped was doing what he was supposed to; his responsibility was to help riders and sweep the course for folks who had broken down and/or needed assistance. That was me. After I headed back into the race, I started to have the feeling that the reason he caught me so quickly was that I was dead last. I did my best to focus on the race ahead, but when I was around the time my first lap was ending, I started to get passed by the folks who were racing for the top of the podium, and already on lap number two. I may have finished last, but I didn't care. The cactus story alone was almost worth the trip from Michigan to Nevada.

But, back at my desk at home, I can easily open another Chrome tab, fill in a few boxes, click a radio button with the amount I want to give, and get right back to work. This is giving, light.

How simple has the internet made all that, and how old do I sound saying that? Online banking is a breeze, paying my monthly credit card takes two minutes, and spending money on big-ticket items is so easy, within five minutes you can buy a motorcycle and have two minutes to spare for the regret to sink in. Apply two cocktails to that formula and it's a right old mess. On a recent birthday, someone neglected to keep me away from my laptop while I was under the influence of a rather abundant amount of both alcohol and Mexican food. It somehow got into my head that I needed a new watch. Now, for the year before this day, the only watch I'd donned was a $35 Timex. I do own an Apple Watch but don't wear it. Some would think my working in technology would cause me to want tech around all the time, but it has had the opposite effect. I stare at enough screens five days a week at my job.

So, on a bright, sunny, beautiful, drunken mid-August day, I ordered an expensive Swiss watch from a boutique jewelry store in London; which cost about the same as my first two motorcycles combined. In my state, I tried to justify it because of a recent pay raise and promotion.

"I earned this, right?" I said out loud as I shut my laptop down after receiving both the confirmation email about the watch order and then the accompanying email from my credit card company regarding the high-dollar charge I just made. After the regret started to sink in, I let out a sigh, then ran away from my laptop as quickly as possible.

This is one of those problems with only having the little devil living on your shoulder. One can only assume he has killed the angel. All I can say is that the angel stormed off after the whole "hey, you really shouldn't rob that bank" incident.

The following day, mildly hungover from the tequila, Mexican Food, and watch purchase, I decided I needed to make a couple of changes in my life. One was to have neither my laptop nor my phone near me when I was drinking, second was to cancel the watch. Done, and done.

I then spent the following day annoyed, and rather revolted at my drunken shopping weakness. I needed to keep an eye on that going forward. I can't say I've been successful, but none of us is perfect. I am sure there's a Bible verse in there if you care to look it up.

I decided to use some of that drunken internet shopping energy to do some good. Or to at least keep me from buying things I didn't need. It sure felt like a win-win kind of operation. But I had one big rule—no telling. It had to be kept in the family.

Sometimes if you seek recognition in life, it can diminish the thing you are doing. Recognition can become a motivation for some people. I wanted us to do something nice for others and forgo the pat on the back.

There's a large rock in front of my daughter's old elementary school; I came up with a plan to surround it with painted rocks. Painted rocks with beautiful colors, painted rocks that had cartoon characters, painted rocks with inspirational messages, and just any old thing we felt like painting. Put a smile on someone's face, that was the only goal.

I'm not a very good artist. It wasn't a gene I either inherited or was able to pass down. My brain never was able to communicate the proper signals to my hands to get them to obey. Creativity I have, just not the skill.

When COVID hit, we got to work. Thankfully, a nearby church had an abundance of landscaping rocks that could provide much of the canvas we would need. Since we weren't taking all that many rocks, my guilt was pretty low. I may be an atheist, but I tend to not be a thief. Seriously, just forget about the bank robbery thing I mentioned earlier.

The family were pretty good sport's about this. The problem was, we approached this from totally different perspectives, me looking for a rock that was shaped like "something" and everyone else needing inspiration before even looking for rocks. We created slogans like "Read!" or "Vote!" or the one time I found a dome-shaped rock painted like Darth Vader's head, did my best to paint it as such, and then wrote "There is good in all of us" on the other side. I was pretty proud of that one. I found a round rock and painted it like a globe, and on a camping trip in the Upper Peninsula of Michigan, I searched the limestone-laden shore for an hour looking for a rock shaped like a piece of pizza. I couldn't find a piece thin enough, so the one I found ended up looking more like a slice of Chicago deep dish.

With the spring turning into summer, we continued to paint rocks and take walks with our clothes weighed down by it all. Often, we'd take the trip over to my daughter's school to find one or two missing. It was mostly the rocks we were proud of that went the quickest. This was fine with us, though, because if someone took the time to look them over and find one they liked, then took it home, we achieved our goal, which was to spread some happiness.

After my daughter returned to in-person school the rock replenishment program slowed to a trickle. Fall turned into winter, and the assumption was that all would soon be buried under snow. I also grew a little tired of doing them all. A family venture turned into a solo project.

One fall morning, I thought we were busted. A family we knew caught me adding a rock to the collection outside her school.

I was bending over, putting a rock on the ground, when a voice behind me said, "You guys adding a rock?"

A mom of a girl in my daughter's class was watching me place the rock on the ground.

"Yeah, thought I would add to the pile," was all I could manage.

"You know," she then stated, "I think we have one or two from here at home. We kept meaning to add some of our own but just never got around to it." I couldn't get anything more coherent out than "Busy… summer… kids…" I'm so bad at human interaction sometimes.

I could have easily told her we did them all, and I kind of wanted to. But people talk, and I didn't want it to come back around to me. That might just lead to me running away if confronted. The goal was to make a few people smile and forget the dark times we were in. I think it was a success.

Later, after COVID restrictions had been lifted, and most people had returned to their normal routines, I revisited the rock-painting topic with a couple of members of my family. The consensus was that this particular time, which I look back on fondly, isn't held in high regard by the other members of my family. One of them uses the acronym "PTSD." This felt a little dramatic, but who am I to tell someone how to feel about a global pandemic? I was surprised, however, that I was the only one who looked back fondly at the rock painting. I am someone who can silo my tasks and don't typically attach sentimentality or emotion to them. It's a blessing and a curse. Mostly a blessing. Might depend on who you ask.

But honestly, that globe rock I painted took me a long time. I kind of want it back.

Where have all my friends gone?

I've lost so many friends over the years. Many of them were gone just as I pushed over the forty-year mark in life.

There was a great unspoken love for someone I was too afraid to seek out. A life cut short by her hand. Our partnership was not to be. She was gone, tragically, alone.

My friend whose physical prowess we were all envious of. He shone too bright for too short of time, leaving so much love and too many holes in too many lives. We all have so many unanswered questions. Too many ribbons on so many great oak trees, faded, windblown, torn.

To my friend who has resided for so many years now in that cemetery in our hometown. He lit up every room he walked into—without saying a word. On that terrible night, he just wasn't able to walk away from the car's twisted wreckage. He died a violent death, befitting a knight in battle. Forever glorious, forever victorious.

My friend, the smart one. So much has already been written about you. How you were robbed of your success, by internal forces. You too battled valiantly, but it was not to be.

My friend, who was the closest thing I had to a sister growing up. We all understood that you needed to leave our circle to create your own. Sadly, the little ones you left behind now only have pictures of you to remember their mom. I hope they grow up knowing about your courage as they forge their own circles.

There is a large maple tree, that sits in my neighbor's yard, adjacent to my home in Ann Arbor. Throughout the year, it drops sticks onto my driveway, and in the fall it drops copious amounts of leaves on my driveway and yard. But, before I can get annoyed by the mess, they are blown away, first into my yard, then into the neighbor's yard, then beyond.

Every year when this happens, it gives me pause. I think about the friends who have come and gone throughout my life. Some are the sticks, which I might pick up and chuck in the compost bin, and some are the leaves, destined to hang around just long enough to be noticed, then sent away by an outside force. This is not unlike my friendships. Some are the sticks, and some are the leaves.

When I wrote this story, it was wintertime in my home state of Michigan. As I looked out over my yard, there were still leaves, dropped down from the neighbor's maple tree. They'd made it through the fall winds and might be around for a while.

I am keeping my eye on them. If they are not worthy, they'll go into the compost bin this spring. If they're lucky, I'll keep them around for a while. But I'm prepared to chuck them all and start over.

When I Flunked out of Band

"What instrument would you like to play?" the middle school band director asked.

"Drums," I replied.

"Oh, sorry, we don't need any more drummers," was his reply.

To this day, I cannot reason why he asked me that question. I didn't have a choice. I was reminded of this not long ago as I was selling off the last of my drum equipment. The guy I had met up with who was buying my kit told me he was a middle school music director, and this memory came flooding back. I blurted out the story as we were loading the drums into his car, and it seemed to give him pause.

"When I started my career, I felt the same way," he told me, laughing, and shaking his head. "But as the years went on, I changed my mind. If a kid came to class with a particular passion for an instrument, I would let them try their hand at it."

Why couldn't this guy have been my band teacher?

"We need trombone players" was what I was told by our band director. Again, why was I even asked? Drums to trombone felt like a total screw job. I gave up before I was even given that silly thing.

I was in my thirties before I picked up the drums as a serious hobby and found out I was right—I could play them. But, this isn't a tale about a wasted skill, or how I could have been something more. Honestly, I just don't get to complain a lot. Also, how many conversations can I work the middle school band into?

So, thanks for listening and letting me grumble.

The Time I Was Shot

The job I held the longest when I lived in Colorado was at an office supply store. It was an okay job, and I made a few friends while working there. One guy had crazy stories about getting several new cars and how within six months of owning them he would be hit by another driver and his brand-new car would be totaled, leaving him to buy another new car. He had told this car story to me, laughing about how through no effort of his own, he had immaculate credit. Crashing cars and constantly paying off their loans will do that, or so that guy said.

Another person I worked with at the office supply store was a former bank teller. I found every aspect of her previous job fascinating. A big factor might have been the fact that I'd watched *Butch Cassidy and the Sundance Kid* over and over during my teen years. I do realize this isn't a very good representation of her job as a teller, since that movie is set around the year 1900. Did they even have dye packs back then? She'd likely not met a lot of other people who found an entry-level position at a bank so interesting, so there were a couple of times she ended her story with, "I probably shouldn't have told you all that." And adding that as a postscript to any story is just the best, isn't it?

One thing she talked to me about was being robbed. She hadn't personally been robbed, but a fellow teller at her bank had been through the ordeal and told her about it. She also filled me in on bank policies and procedures regarding robberies. Oh, and about how the dye pack mechanism worked. Again, too much information was supplied by her, to me. She was a chatty gal. *If* I remembered her name, I would withhold it. But I don't, so I can't, so I won't.

A person walks up to your window, points a gun at you, and hands you a note. You're supposed to simply hand the money over. The last thing the bank wants is for someone to get shot (and the teller too, of course). The money isn't worth risking your life for, or any of your vital organs. This leads me to the question: Can you rob a bank with a pellet gun? Bank policy prohibits employees from acting like heroes. Just hand over the money, they say. Just hand over the money. Oh, and slip in a dye pack if possible.

Circling back to the pellet gun, while dropping the bank robber theme temporarily. Let's say someone points one at you. Maybe that person is your brother. Then maybe your pellet gun-wielding brother tells you to move out of the way. Surely, he wouldn't shoot you, as sure as the bank teller is of *their* safety, right? Neither my brother nor the robber has the incentive to shoot. The robber wants money, my brother just wants his annoying little brother to move. Just hand over the money. And the dye pack.

I bring up the pellet gun incident for a reason. Or, the day my brother shot me, or that day when I almost lost my left eye, or that wasted summer after my brother shot me in the eye with that pellet gun, (that bastard) incident.

It was forty years ago that this took place. I have a vivid memory of where we were standing and what was around me at the time. It's one of the most vivid memories I have from childhood.

At this time in our lives, we had a babysitter during the summer since my mother worked days, and we were not old or mature enough to be home alone. She was a teenage girl from the neighborhood, and she was roughly fifteen at the time. Like many babysitters, she was just there to make sure we didn't do something stupid like burning the house down or shooting someone's eye out. I remember her name being Dawn and I also remember she was obsessed with the soap opera actor turned-rock star Rick Springfield. If I'm skewing too old here, you'll have to Google him. He was (and perhaps still is) a handsome fella.

At some point in our childhood, my brother acquired a pellet gun. Who knows how young boys get these things? Things get left behind, items are traded away because one kid or another used them to kill a squirrel, a bird, etc., and then there comes a need to shift the evidence. You know, the usual boy stuff. A pellet gun, for those not familiar, is like a BB gun, but with different ammo.

BB gun ammo is a small steel ball, while pellet gun ammo would have been made out of lead forty years ago and has more of a domed shape, a slightly pointy mushroom-looking thing. The pellet gun my brother had in his possession wouldn't be in his possession long.

The story goes, we were playing outside on a beautiful summer's day when I became an obstacle. I was in the firing line that day and would pay for my insolence.

"Move," my brother ordered.

"No way," I ignorantly stated.

"I'm warning you!" came the threat from my brother.

"No."

"I'll shoot you," came his final warning.

"You wouldn't dare," I spat.

The next thing I knew, I was hit and then doubled over. He had hit me near my left eye but was unaware of the damage that it had done.

"I told you to move," my brother triumphantly retorted.

He walked over to me, making sure I wasn't playing possum, and when I took my hand away from my face, all the while complaining about how he shot me, I could see the fear in his eyes. He looked more shocked than I had the time I crashed the mower through the screen door.

"Let's get you a towel to put on that," he said, sounding worried.

I was oblivious and not in much pain and we ran inside to get a towel and some ice to put on my wound. My brother winced as I took my hand away and then winced again as he filled the towel with ice and I placed it back on my left eye. My vision out of the eye was almost non-existent. Even I began to worry at this point.

"Maybe we should go tell Dawn," my brother said, the worry still clear in his voice.

If the babysitter needed to be told, maybe this was worse than I had feared. She was in my mom's room watching some sort of soap opera, as one would in the mid-1980s. There wasn't much else on TV in the middle of the day. I dare to say that there was *nothing* else on weekdays during the day.

I burst into the room and over to her, my panic now reaching a tipping point between the kitchen and the bedroom. I ran around the side of the bed to where she was sitting. As the room was laid out, there was a large vanity directly across from me on the opposite wall.

"Brian shot me!" I blurted out to Dawn.

"Let me see," she said, sitting up.

I then removed the towel from my face, now seeing some blood on the towel, but instead of looking down at her, I glanced up into the large mirror on top of the vanity across the room. Through my increasingly blurry vision, I could tell it didn't look good. That, mixed with the blood, tipped me into freaking-the-fuck-out mode.

Dawn leaped to her feet and into action. Did she learn stuff like this in babysitter class, I would wonder later in life? I started to fade off into the gray as I now sat on the edge of the bed, Dawn frantically making phone calls. She wasn't old enough to drive, so we were going to have to get help some other way. I was then hurried through the house, and then out the front door. My gray was fading into a dark gray by now, and I was losing track of my surroundings. As Dawn rushed me down the driveway, a car suddenly stopped in the middle of our road at the end of the driveway, but I didn't have any idea who it was. I was shoved into the back seat, and my charcoal gray faded off to black. I was heading… somewhere.

There were only brief glimpses while I was at the hospital for the next couple of hours. I seemed to go in and out of consciousness. A glimpse of a doctor, my brother, my mother.

"Stitches," I heard the doctor say. Also, something to the effect, "you were lucky you didn't lose your left eye."

The part of my eye that the pellet hit was called the Dennie-Morgan lines. These are the folds that are just below the eye, something I have more of now than I did when I was a kid. If you push this skin just below the eye, you can feel your actual eye behind it. That's how close it was. I will give you a second to try it on yourself. The pellet had managed to pass through the skin but not make it to my eye. Not the first, nor the last stroke of luck that would find its way into my life.

For several weeks after the incident, I was physically a mess. I am not aware of why it had such a profound effect on my well-being, but it did. I spent day after day in bed, at first not being able to see out of either eye for the first few days home from the hospital, then slowly being able to watch television for short periods. My summer was being washed away by my blurry-to-no vision, and my brother's possibly good, or bad aim.

Young boys are often turds to each other, especially if they are siblings. My brother didn't intentionally send me to the hospital bleeding all over some nice neighbor's car. Then did anything provoke this? I dare say it was revenge. It was a diabolical plan hatched months before by the shooter, my only brother. Revenge was executed on me for a careless and entirely intentional act I performed upon him. There was a fracas that involved a game, which involved marbles, which led to me throwing a marble directly at him, and resulted in the tooth and a trip to the dentist.

I do not doubt that Step A of his plan started that day. Sure, he might not have known this would involve a pellet gun since he didn't have it in his possession at that time, but the seed of vengeance was planted. Are we talking about an eye for an eye biblical stuff? Of course not. Just, a seed.

While my brother lost an afternoon because of a trip to the dentist, I lost a large chunk of my summer break from school, laid up in bed, not being able to properly see. Swelling and all the meds were the main cause of my ailing. All the meds were to help the infection and combat the pain, but the side effects kicked my ass. I was half-blind and constantly nauseous.

As discussed briefly earlier, this was the mid-1980s, and television had a long way to go. Daytime television had long since been taken over by soap operas, and little else was on. You had a total of four channels to occupy your time. There was fuck-all on.

If you think watching soap operas is bad enough, think of lying in bed listening to them. It's a cheesy audiobook, with bad dialog and worse music.

With a portion of my summer ruined, I was on the mend and was finally able to get outside. There were to be no daredevil bike stunts performed for the rest of the summer. No riding down Big Bertha, no riding across the creek, and absolutely no racing friends down the neighborhood boulevard. I was on low-key restriction until school started back up.

My brother, by the time I was mended, had had his grounding, and his reprimand, and with his vengeance set upon me, the score between us sat 1-1. My eye was healing, and no long-term damage was detected. Many years later, I would come to believe that this incident had done something to me emotionally, long term.

In my thirties, I lived with a woman who at the time was a federal officer. I came to understand that I was uneasy around her firearm. I had very little exposure to firearms before this time in my life, so I think that was why it took me so long to realize my nervousness. On one occasion, she called me after leaving our apartment to ask if I would put her service weapon away in the safe. She had hastily left it out after getting home from work and hanging her belt and holstered weapon up on the closet door. I unholstered her weapon and placed it in the safe as she asked me to, unquestionably violating several departmental policies. Gun advocates might say I am uncomfortable with firearms because of my limited experience. I would argue, that is *not* the cause.

The score between my brother and I is no longer 1-1. I implemented a new scoring system, many years ago. I was keeping count until around five years ago when the score was so one-sided that it no longer made sense to keep track of who had what. This has become a one-horse race, with me not even bothering to attend the race.

You see, every time my brother has had a leaky roof, a flat tire, bed bugs, icy sidewalks, missing tools, unexpected visits from the police, incorrect take-out orders, missing socks, missing food from his refrigerator, missing money, and so many other things, he has considered it back luck. At this point, I am hoping he believes he's cursed. I assure you, he is not. Every penny I have spent paying off pizza delivery drivers, every late night I've had skulking around his house, poking holes in his garden hose-it's all been worth it.

My life hasn't turned into a competition, it *is* a competition. One that will not only cost my daughter her college tuition but will one day likely claim my life. Headline: "Man Dies After Decades-Old Prank Goes Awry."

There Is NO Cursing on any Channel

I was recently reminded of the time during my teens when some friends and I gathered around midnight to drive from our small town in southeastern Michigan to a town called South Haven, which lies on the shores of Lake Michigan, simply for a swim.

I don't remember which one of us initially had the idea to go or how we ended up with two cars, and five people, all willing participants. After we were all gathered, we set off.

As I have mentioned before, most teens will find any excuse to drive around. What could be a better reason than to go for a swim? No pool is open twenty-four hours, and we did live in a state with an abundance of lakes. It made all the sense in the world.

This was long before cell phones, and taking two cars seemed a little silly until one among us suggested using walkie-talkies during the trip there and back. Since the rendezvous point was the guy who had all the equipment lying around, what did we have to lose? Our friend's father owned a sprinkler system installation business, and he must have purchased all this equipment to communicate with the guys out in the field. Though, this was just a guess. Sometimes people just buy stuff like that for fun.

After all the equipment was dragged out and thrown into the middle of the room it reminded me of the sight I might see if a Radio-Shack had just exploded-shit, have I used that joke before? Enough cords to tie end to end and escape from prison, so many different-sized antennas that one would assume you'd need two to make the thing work, and several mountable base units, which I certainly wouldn't be mounting inside my Nissan Sentra. I'm pretty sure no one had any idea how it worked, but walkie-talkies, or CB Radios as I'll call them from here on out—are pretty self-explanatory. The antenna, power, and mic thing all have different ends, so there's little guesswork. Nearly teenage-proof.

The CB's were installed into/onto the two cars, and we were ready to roll. It was 1 a.m., and we were setting off for our five-to-six-hour roundtrip journey. Like many things teens do, this made so little sense that it wasn't even thoroughly discussed. Just an excuse to hit the road.

We made innocent chatter on the trip: jokes, stories, terrible singalongs, nothing more unusual than things you'd be doing on a family road trip. What we failed to understand was that CBs are a pretty open medium. As we trundled on toward the lake, we began to annoy our fellow CB users, mainly truckers. I can only speak for myself, but I had no idea others could hear our chatter until an unknown voice came over the CB stating, "Could you guys just give it a rest?"

This was followed by several seconds of silence from our end while we processed what we'd heard, and only then did it dawn on us that the semi-trucks within some particular distance could hear everything. This is where an explicative was blurted out by us, over the CB.

"There's no cursing over the radio" rang out in both our cars.

Silence.

"Let's switch channels," came over the CB from our friends in the other car.

"There's no cursing on any channel," the semi-driver then reported.

Again, silence.

We gave it a rest for a few minutes, switched channels, then scaled back our hijinks for the remainder of the trip, doing our best to lay off the curse words on the new channel. There was no real reason to piss off the semi-drivers in our immediate vicinity. Hell, we didn't even know there were rules on CB use. What we didn't know was that the Federal Communications Commission CB Rule 13 states that you cannot transmit obscene, indecent, or profane words. But, what ignorant teenager knows that?

The rest of the trip out went quickly, and we soon found ourselves in the city of South Haven, Michigan, navigating our crew to the lake. It was still dark, but the sun would be lighting things up in a short while. One of the guys in our group had spent some time in South Haven wooing a local gal, so for some reason, we thought he could navigate toward the lake. Just keep heading west, right? We circled blocks and drove in the wrong direction repeatedly, enough so that some of us wondered why we'd decided to do this in the first place. But, finally, we spotted the beach, found parking, and all breathed a sigh of relief. Towels gathered up, we stepped out of the cars, stretched, and took three steps toward the beach before a police officer rolled up. You see, two cars caravanning around the small beach town of South Haven in the early hours couldn't help but draw attention. After a very short inquiry, the bravest of us spoke up.

"We drove here to jump in the lake," one of our group stated.

"The five of you drove from where to jump in the lake?" the officer asked with a very quizzical look on his face.

"Adrian," we all replied in unison.

"Adrian? Where is that?" The officer was not amused with our teenage road trip to his town.

"We've been driving for more than three hours, officer," was our retort.

"Well, you've wasted a trip—I can't let you guys go over there," he said, pointing toward the beach.

We were crestfallen. Our hopes were crushed. We'd just driven hours only to be denied entry. Thwarted by the authorities, again. With no other choice, we piled back into the cars and set off for home. At the time, it seemed so unfair. Even if the officer had allowed us five minutes to dip our toes in the water, the trip would have felt worth it.

The trip was exhausting, and we all struggled on the drive back. The CB and all the games, singalongs, and foolishness we had enjoyed on the trip out just left us annoyed now. Hungry, tired, and defeated we just headed back, thinking only of bed.

For much of my life, I've come up with my share of high-risk crazy ideas, often dragging someone along, generally with mediocre success. They have ranged from the small-scale lake drive to much larger, life-changing-sized ideas. Need a few examples? Not too long after this failed lake idea, I convinced one of the guys on that trip to drive from Michigan to Miami, Florida, to watch a football game. It was the twilight years of football greats Dan Marino and Joe Montana and they were likely playing each other for the last time. So, we drove the 1,200 miles for a three-hour football game, and pretty much had the worst seats in the stadium.

Opportunity is often the catalyst for many of these sill ideas. I approached my friend Dave years ago about going to Dublin, Ireland so we could visit the Guinness beer factory to have a pint, from the source. We *did* go, and it was fantastic.

A little more recently, on a random Tuesday, I got in my head that I wanted to visit a brewery I was quite fond of near the upper Michigan lakeside town of Traverse City. Other than the beer, they had a couple of dishes I enjoyed. It went from a random thought to obsession in a matter of hours. By the end of the day, I had two nights booked for the coming weekend at a beachside hotel. Again, worth it.

Before I had a family, spur-of-the-moment motorcycle trips were the norm, though they sometimes came with a cost. On one occasion, I decided to do some camping in Canada, but when I showed up at the Detroit-to-Windsor tunnel entrance, they informed me no motorcycles were permitted and I'd have to navigate my way back to the bridge and take that over to Canada.

Light planning combined with poor execution is how I tend to see the world and my navigation of it. I always thought I could see the possibilities laid out before me, and often I have considered this my responsibility, to open others' eyes to my worldview. Planning every detail of a vacation can lead to having a narrow view of adventure, or not even understanding what adventure might mean.

If I were to read an article about some bar closing that had been making the best espresso martini in the world, I'd book a flight. If I am on a trip and find out there's a Civil War battlefield two hours away, I'll make the trek over there to see it. I've never been hesitant to book a flight, a train ticket, or a hotel, with two days' lead time.

So many of us will sit on our porches and watch the world roll by. Who knows better than me what I need? No travel agent or website can build me an adventure. It must be fluid, and I need to be handed the levers of control, though often loosely.

I have created an adventure/vacation spreadsheet, to which anyone can be added, and which is updated often. The items on the list range from a multi-day hike on Vancouver Island to a weekend trip on a houseboat down the Mississippi River.

In the future, I plan on sending out pay-as-you-go cell phones to all those I share the spreadsheet with, so with the narrowest of windows they can grab their bags, head out their doors, and be off with me. Adventure awaits, for the daring, and the stupid.

Through the Picket Lines

In between the vomiting, I held your hand.

I was not there for the actual procedure, I wasn't

allowed. I just drove the car that got us there.

They say two people make a child, but from time to

time it takes only one to let it go.

We were warned there would be picketers, and there

were.

At times we were at odds when discussing options.

I did not beg, but maybe I should have.

We loved each other, and we could make it through

this.

We were too young, someone said.

We didn't have the right jobs, the right education, or

the right healthcare plan available.

Maybe a time would come when we could have another.

You looked so sad that day.

Did we tell our families about where we were that day?

Who would we call in an emergency?

When it was over, I held your hand, remember?

Someone called you a baby killer.

We were able to keep our relationship going, for a while.

You looked so sad that day...

The whole story behind that was a complicated one, as countless emotional tales naturally are. Telling this story in a single creative writing style seemed impossible to me. There are too many feelings locked away about this. I must continue to hold bits back, for my sake and for others who were involved.
I am a closed book for a reason.

Here is another version.

In my early twenties, my girlfriend at the time became pregnant. At that time we lived, together, we loved each other, and I even think we planned on spending our lives together. But after discussing the matter a few times, a decision was made that she would get an abortion. I don't remember how many talks we had surrounding this. How could I? It was so many years ago now.

I was torn. On the one hand, we were employed and had an apartment, cars, and health insurance, but we were scared and poor. She was born to an upper-class family, so having a child at a young age without "means" was rather unacceptable. Get your schooling done, get your career going, and then procreate. I knew the conditions weren't perfect, but my youth made me optimistic, and probably a little foolish. I thought we could make it work. Difficult life conditions make you who you are. Even today being someone who tends to calculate risk for most decisions he makes, this made me uneasy and landed me in some gray zone I tended not to venture into very often.

At the end of the day, I didn't feel like it was in my power to push for a decision I wanted. I loved her and would stick by her and help her get through *whatever* choice was made.

So, on a Saturday that started no different than any other, we found ourselves in the saddest waiting room you will ever want to encounter. This was far darker than the time you might spend waiting for the funeral director to collect you. This was a room filled with people who have all decided to make a tough choice—for most, the toughest decision they may ever make in their lives. Just to walk through the door in the morning took more courage than I thought I possessed. It was only having each other that day that allowed us to get up that morning, drive over to the clinic, and get through their door.

After an agonizing wait, she was called back, and I was alone. To wait, alone. To wonder, alone. I just stared at the floor, tracing the lines in the carpet with my eyes, until they led me too close to another human. I would then start back at the lines around my feet and work my way outward. *Don't look at anyone*, I thought.

After some time, I was called back. The physical portion of this terrible day was ending, which would lead us to some form of emotional healing. Later, I would find myself wishing I had carpet lines to trace, coveting solitude from this burden I didn't want to shoulder. We didn't talk much about that day, and I do my best not to think of it. It is too dark to return there, the pain endures, and the emotional healing persists.

To My Future Self

I recently unearthed a time capsule, buried in the backyard at my childhood home. Don't worry, I got permission from the current owners.

Here is the gist of it:

I have made a list of things to remember, which will help you in your life in the busy city. I have also made a list of cool questions for you to answer. But since this will be in the past, you can't write me back. Time travel is really confusing.

- Say goodbye to Mom, Dad, or both when you leave for work every morning. I'm sure they live next door.

- Don't forget to refuel your jetpack.

- Make sure your butler does the dishes. I know you hate doing the dishes.

- Don't forget to go to the comic shop to get the new Thor. I bet he's still your favorite comic book character.

- Remember to always tell Grandma and Grandpa "thank you" even when they just buy you dumb old socks for Christmas.

- Are Michael Jackson and Prince still making music? All the kids tell me I can't like both, but I do.

- Are you still the fastest kid in the neighborhood?

- Have you seen the Titanic? They are talking about raising it now they have located it. That would be so cool. Maybe you got to go on it?

- Did you ever beat that Commodore 64 game called: A Bard's Tale? I hope you did; it was sooooo hard.

- Did our neighbor Angie ever catch you? She used to chase us on the playground and said we'd have to marry her if she caught us. I hope she didn't.

- Did Mom and Dad stop fighting all the time?

- Are Moon Boots still popular? I've only got a pair of old hand-me-downs from Brian. They smelled really bad.

- When someone invents the time machine, please come back and visit me.

Travel Diary – A Solo Adventure

"Mr. Brad, your drink."

My hesitation in responding to this announcement stems from my desire to finish the sentence on the page in front of me. A couple of seconds felt like an eternity.

"Sorry, thank you, Samuel."

I could tell it was him. Throughout my short time here, I have become familiar with this man, Samuel. He quickly felt like an old friend and confidant, and when Samuel sends me an email in a year to ask how I am doing, it doesn't feel strange, or meddlesome. He was my salvation on that trip. He, after all, was one of the first people I encountered on my trip down to the Blue Haven Resort.

But, let's start from the beginning.

The front desk was nothing if not professional and courteous as they inconspicuously glanced over my shoulder at check-in. Since the suite was booked for two people, they were curious about when the other member of my party was going to walk through the door.

"Is the other party running late, Mr. Poore?"

"Fraid not. Party of one this trip." My failure to sound upbeat was my tell.

"No problem Mr. Poore. Please let us know if you need anything during your stay."

I was handed the key to suite 206 after a barrage of thank yous and apologies from me, for what I wasn't even sure about, and I was off to my room. But just for long enough to set my backpack down before a much-needed trip to the bar and then the beach. I packed what would fit into my travel backpack-two pairs of shorts, three shirts, underwear, no socks, a couple of my favorite books, and a few toiletries. More than enough to sit by the beach, drink, and eat.

My room was gorgeous, an airy one-bedroom, second-floor suite with a balcony overlooking the white sand beach and brilliant blue water that surrounds Turks and Caicos. I stood on the balcony, my backpack slung over my shoulder. The view was right, but everything else was wrong.

I left the balcony, walked back into my room, and pulled a book out of my backpack—my entertainment, and not factoring in the alcohol, was my only escape this trip. I tucked it under my arm with little in mind other than making my way to the bar, then to a lounge chair on the beach.

Not knowing the lay of the land, I headed back to the kind front desk staff, assuming they could point me in the correct direction.
"Salt Bar is on your way to the beach, or there's a bar in the pool if you prefer, Mr. Poore."
"Perfect, thank you," I said, and I wandered off in the direction the woman had been gesturing.

I saw a sign for the Salt Bar twenty feet from the front desk and made my way inside. It was late afternoon, still sometime before a normal dinner time, and apparently after all the old folks had eaten, leaving the Salt Bar almost empty when I arrived. I had no desire to eat food. I'd forced down breakfast and some Oreos on the plane ride down here. It's hard for me to pass up first-class meals. I always found them delicious.

"Hello sir, how are you today?"

"Fine, thanks. Two vodka and cranberries, with a slice of lime on the rim, please." No pleasantries today. I just didn't have it in me. I'd been so glad when my seatmate on the plane got on and immediately put his headphones on. I was so relieved.

"Yes sir, coming right up."

I turned around and walked a few steps closer to the door, which led out to the lounge chairs and beach area and where my salvation lay. This also had the effect of insulating me from unwanted chit-chat. Before my brain could ramble its way onto Marcy, my drinks were ready.

"Sir?"

Strolling over to the bar to accept them, I could see salvation within reach.

"On your room, sir?"

"Please. Room 206."

I set a ten-dollar bill on the counter before picking up my drinks. I never understood why a British territory used the US dollar as its currency. Therefore, I freely admit my ignorance—probably a conscious decision to forgo a career in finance, or whatever line of work deals with counting, sorting, minting, trading, or even the history of money.

I headed for the door and was immediately thrilled to have been served my drinks in Collins glasses. Think tall and thin (like me) instead of short and round (like Marcy). Navigating doors with a book and two cocktails was tricky, at least for me. If the glasses were too big around, I couldn't hold them both in one hand, which would leave me scrambling to open doors with one finger. And let's not even throw a book into that equation. The time I start using my book as a bar tray I could kiss those drinks goodbye. Thankfully, Collins glasses *are* the perfect circumference for carrying multiple at once.

It was an easy walk after that difficulty from the bar out to the beach. With no one around I chose a lounge chair, kicked off my Vans, and settled in. The Vans, a gift from Marcy, were removed with a mixture of satisfaction and pain.

I shoved one of my cocktails into a shady spot in the sand, and put my book on my lap. I contemplated opening it but couldn't manage anything other than staring out to sea—unless you count sipping on my drink. I continued to glance down at my book. I'd brought down my battered *and* well-read first edition of John Le Carré's *Tinker, Tailor, Soldier, Spy*. I think I chose this book because I already knew how it ended. Predictable. There could be a metaphor inserted here, but there was too much drinking still to be done.

I finished off my first cocktail setting it down in a cool patch of sand, provided by the large umbrella shading me from the sun. I picked up my second drink.

I'd considered being contemplative about the situation, but every time I formed a thought another wave came in and washed it away. I loved the effect the sea (or is it the ocean?) has on me. Marcy always hated that about the sea.

"It's too oppressive" she'd always say.

That day, that's exactly what I needed. Oppress my brain. All thoughts would be extinguished by the ocean, and alcohol. Every time my brain wandered to thoughts of the mid-winter Michigan weather, Marcy, our pets, or my job, it was gone again, washed away. I might be finally able to find some peace in my life, albeit in an impractical, *very* expensive way.

I grabbed *Tinker, Tailor, Soldier, Spy* from the sand, shook it off, turned it over a couple of times in my hand, then set it back down. It could just end up being a coaster for today. Now two-thirds of the way through my second cocktail, I began to enjoy some mild-fuzziness settling in.

"Mr. Poore?" Someone had approached from behind, and I didn't notice.

"Yeah. Hi." I glanced up at this man. He bent down to pick up my empty cocktail glass, and I was then able to bring him into focus.

"Another vodka and cranberry with a lime wedge, Mr. Poore? Or, perhaps, two?"

The waiter was tall, and thin, with light brown perfect skin and an accent I couldn't quite place. French? The island of Saint-Martin is one of a handful of French territories in the Caribbean. So, I went with that.

"One, please, just a second."

I put the straw to my lips and sucked down the rest of my drink with one long pull. He then reached down with a smile on his face and took the second glass from me.

"Thank you," I say, looking up at him.

"Sir," he says, pivoting then walking away and back toward the hotel.

I reach down and grab my book, shook the sand off once again, before settling it onto my lap. I've decided to try and read until the waiter returns. My focus is still pretty shaky but, it's worth a try.

A few pages were all I managed before he returned, my lone drink on his tray. This time, when I glance up at him it dawns on me that this man was there when I checked in. The woman who checked me in was in the middle of a conversation when I walked up. This is the man she was talking to. "Your vodka and cranberry with a lime wedge, sir. I'll come back and check on you in a little bit Mr. Poore, to see if you need another drink or a menu."

"Call me Brad, please," I plead while accepting my drink from him.

"Yes sir, Mr. Brad, will do."

We were both smiling as he turned to go. I should have expected that. I took a sip, slipped my bookmark into my book, and closed it. Reading for more than a minute or two at a time just seemed futile. On my best days, I wasn't able to accomplish anything of importance after two cocktails. I was even semi-worthless after one.

I take a long draw from my straw, and my mind wanders to Marcy. I fight it like hell, but the ocean sound fades, and only thoughts of her are left in my head.

Marcy, who is supposed to be with me.
Marcy, who is probably packing her belongings at our home right now.
Marcy, who walked out after a fight, got into her car, and drove out into a snowstorm.

I strained my focus back onto the brilliant blue ocean in front of me. A couple with their child seemingly has come out of nowhere and walked between the end of my chair and the water. Probably in their late thirties with a child around eight. I didn't follow them with my gaze. They became a blur in my peripherals, then disappeared altogether. There was no space for strangers. I'm too busy trying not to make space for Marcy. At least until the ocean was able to take back over.

I stared down at my drink and swirled my ice around. Only ice is left. I feel the slight resistance from the ice cubes as my straw sends them racing around the bottom of the glass. Around, and around. I can't hear the clinking over the ocean, but I know it must be there.

"Hello, Mr. Brad."

I glanced up, smiling. My salvation had returned.

"I didn't catch your name, sorry."

"Samuel, sir. Another cocktail, Mr. Brad? Perhaps you want to see a menu?"

"Please. Both, Samuel."

"For sure Mr. Brad," he said with a smile that I convinced myself must be genuine.

Four drinks are *really* pushing it for me. I am pleasant after one, cheerful at two, a little too talkative after three, and out and out depressed at four. I handed Samuel my third empty glass and he nodded and walked off toward the hotel.

Marcy, who I called and texted that night of the snowstorm, for hours.
Marcy, who didn't let me know she was okay, and not in a ditch.
Marcy, who didn't tell me the real reason for walking out.

Shit. I lay back on the lounge chair and pulled my feet out of the sun. My legs and feet hadn't seen the sun in months, and I didn't want to be both hungover and sunburned the following morning.

Marcy, who was safe and warm in someone else's house the night of that snowstorm.
Marcy, who was not in a ditch or asleep in her car.
Marcy, who had a friend from work I didn't know anything about.

"Your drink, and menu Mr. Brad."

"Thank you, Samuel. If you don't mind, can I just take a quick look and tell you what I want? It won't take me long, just a second."

"Of course, Mr. Brad."

I looked for the appetizer portion of the menu and quickly decided. I then spotted the word "pizza" on the menu but fought off the urge. All that dough would soak up *some* of the alcohol, but I'd probably get screwed with a thin-crust pizza.

"I'll take the Kobe Beef Sliders please, Samuel."

"Very good, Mr. Brad. I'll bring those out shortly."

"Oh, and a glass of water please, Samuel."

My focus waned, again. He had a kind face. The alcohol is giving him that Vaseline-over-the-camera-lens feel they used to use on female movie stars. Think Cybill Shepherd in *Moonlighting*.

I picked up my book, gave it a shake, and began again on page four. I was a paragraph in before I glanced back up toward the ocean. I closed it and tossed it back onto the sand. I stared out at the waves as they rolled in, absentmindedly swirling my straw around in my glass. I couldn't tell if it was the alcohol or my situation making me so melancholy. How could one ever exist without the other?

Marcy, who professed her love and honesty to me.
Marcy, who took the ring from the box and told me we'd always be together.
Marcy, who let the planning go on.

Another couple is walking by, two kids in tow. I smile and nod after they say hello. I watch the back of them for a few more seconds and hoped they were unhappy. Four drinks, depressed. Four drinks, all have played a part in my destruction, except Samuel.

Me, who let the planning go on.
Me, who had his great-grandmother's ruby removed from the only piece of jewelry she carried on her long and arduous journey to this country, set into the engagement ring.

Me, who held on too tight.

I heard laughing behind me and glanced over my shoulder toward the hotel. A couple is at the poolside bar. I hope they're miserable too. Four drinks, obstinate. Four drinks, they're all culpable. But before I can swing my gaze back toward the ocean, I saw Samuel emerge from the hotel, carrying a tray. Shit, maybe I am hungry. Was that out loud? I gave Samuel a wave and a smile and turned back toward the water. Damn, I spun around too fast. A few seconds later, he was at my side.

"Kobe Beef Sliders, and a glass of water, Mr. Brad."

I set my legs on either side of the lounge chair, and Samuel set the tray down where my feet were.

"Anything else, Mr. Brad?"

"No thank you, Samuel, nothing for now."

He hesitated as I glanced down at the cocktail in my hand. All the swirling has melted the ice and dampened my progress on the fourth drink. I didn't need another. Samuel seems to have measured my drunkenness accurately and thinks better of offering me a fifth cocktail.

"I'll come back and check on you soon, Mr. Brad."

Before he'd finished that last sentence, I grabbed a slider and took a bite.

"Fank-oo," I say through a mouthful of Kobe Beef, brioche, sautéed onions, and blue cheese. Four drinks, obnoxious. Four drinks, overwhelming sadness.

I devoured the four sliders and downed my glass of water. I ate so fast that when I looked down at the empty plate, I wondered if a bird had swiped one.

"I could use some dessert," I say out loud and to no one in particular. After four drinks, I was unable to discern between internal and external dialog any longer.

"Why," I start, but then the thought is lost.

"Mr. Brad, how are we?"

Fuck, did he hear me?

Samuel's back, and just in time. Any longer and I would have begun that conversation with myself.

"Dessert, Samuel, I require some dessert."

I was three and a half drinks in, but I think the food and time have allowed the slipping back to two and a half. My gloominess was lifted, and I had made my way back to chatty.

"Sure thing Mr. Brad, let me get the dessert menu, but I'm quite partial to the Espresso Crème Brûlée."

"Perfect, I'll take it!" I exclaimed in my overly animated drunken enthusiasm.

"Any coffee? Tea? Brandy? Mr. Brad?

I glanced down at my drink. I would have been mad to order a fifth.

"Coffee Americano, please Samuel."

Shit, Marcy, the two of us sitting at a café in Dublin. Pull it together.

"Sure thing, Mr. Brad."

Samuel leaves and for the first time I pondered sobering up. But who was I kidding, I wouldn't be sobering up for days. I had six more of them ahead of me.

Me, who was too out of his league with Marcy to notice.
Me, who refused to see the truth.
Me, who didn't have the right friends to ward him off Marcy.

Awaiting my dessert, I turned back to John Le Carré. But, after a paragraph, I flung it onto the sand. I am suddenly overwhelmed. The hotel's sixteen lounge chairs became the focus of my ire. Sixteen, eight pairs, mocking me, two-by-two. I was the only hotel guest out there. I finish off my fourth drink with fervor, I swung my legs over the right side of the lounge chair and kicked the chair next to me. It was too damn close. I eyed the hotel doors, and thankfully Samuel wasn't on his way out here to see this. He undoubtedly saw me at my worst, and semi-best, for those days.

I set my empty glass in the sand, stood up, walked around the other side of the chair next to me, and pulled it away from where I'm sitting. "Fucking couples" I spat. Dammit, I'm doing it, again.

Try to keep it in your head.

I dragged it over and made a trio with a couple of other chairs. I peeked up at the hotel and Samuel is on his way back. Since he was present at my check-in there's no doubt he knew there was something up with me. Hurriedly went back to my lounge chair.

I better apologize. What ego you must have, to think the staff is talking about you, empathizing with you. Like you weren't the cause.

"Espresso Crème Brûlée and Coffee Americano, Mr. Brad." I again made space for Samuel to set the tray on my chair.

"Thanks, Samuel. And sorry I moved the lounge chair, I hope it's ok."

"No problem at all, Mr. Brad," Samuel says with an airy wave of the hand. And he makes believe that *it is* indeed, okay. "Anything else, Mr. Brad?"

"Oh yes, one more thing." Samuel hadn't moved a muscle, but I said it with a sense of urgency in my voice. "Could I please get three fingers of Grand Marnier? If you have it?"

"No problem, Mr. Brad I'll be back shortly."

Marcy, whose maid of honor and bridesmaids had already purchased their dresses.

Marcy, who would receive texts from a number I didn't recognize telling her she was beautiful.

Marcy, who knew how much I liked crème brûlée.

The dessert and coffee were delightful but brought me no joy. Drinking strong, hot coffee on the beach doesn't make any sense. Reminded me of the time I sat out at a Starbucks in the dead of summer and enjoyed a coffee, only to figure out my loopiness afterward was caused by sunstroke.

"Why the fuck didn't I order actual food," I said, looking down at the empty ramekin the crème brûlée once filled. One last sip of coffee, and as I pulled the cup away Samuel is there, holding a tray with a single glass that contained three fingers of a thick orange-colored liquid.

"Your Grand Marnier, Mr. Brad. And let me clear these dishes away."

I took the glass from Samuel, and he picked up my empty coffee cup and ramekin.

"Anything else at the moment, Mr. Brad?" Samuel says with as genuine of a smile as I've seen all day.

"No thank you, Samuel. I appreciate it."

Me, who will come home to an empty house.
Me, who will never get over this disappointment.
Me, who will drown his sorrow with alcohol, until it kills him.

I glanced down at *Tinker, Tailor, Soldier, Spy,* again, but I couldn't pick it up. I held my drink in my lap with both hands, and hoped it would extinguish some life force, if held tight enough. If held with enough care. Part of me was enjoying the sick anticipation of the glass collapsing between my fingers. Cutting me. Providing some relief. If only briefly. More than four drinks, semi-conscious.

The ocean continued to swim in and out of focus with every sip I took from my glass. My eyes were now shifting left and right, which is a sign of nothing good to come. I put my head back and closed my eyes. That might be even worse. I focused on the sound of the waves and the glass between my fingers. *I should order more food, maybe a main, and a salad. Just focus on the ocean,* I told myself.

"Mr. Brad?" Samuel is back and I lazily tipped my head forward and opened my eyes.

"My apologies for disturbing you, but the tide is coming in. This is the time of day we move the lounge chairs back."

"Sure, okay, no problem," I said, finishing with a grunt as I struggle physically, and emotionally, to my feet.

"Thank you, Mr. Brad." And Samuel went off to start at the end of the row.

I threw *Tinker, Tailor, Soldier, Spy* on the chair, and feebly dragged my lounge chair back while keeping an eye on how far Samuel was moving the chairs. Most important of all, I am needed to keep my drink upright. I looked like a blind man driving a tow truck that only has three wheels. I dragged the chair back in fits and starts and it takes me as long to do my chair as Samuel has taken to do ten.

"Thank you, Mr. Brad," Samuel said as he walked past me to do the rest.

Failing to be of any actual help, I collapsed back down into my lounge chair and sipped my drink.

"Anything else you need right now, Mr. Brad?" Samuel asked me walking back to my side.

"I might need some more food, Samuel." It came out of my mouth loosely, and with every intention of not slurring his name, I fail.

"I'll go grab you a menu, Mr. Brad."

"Thanks, Samuel." It's all I managed to get out.

I sunk once again into the recesses of my lounge chair. The ocean is blurry beyond my feet, my John Le Carré book nestled between them.

Marcy, who through streaming tears continued to profess her love to me even after the wedding had been canceled.

Me, who is on his honeymoon, alone.

Samuel, who is the only person in my life who matters.

Whose Car Keys Are Those?

Why would anyone leave their keys in their car overnight? Just sitting inside the car, not even hidden. Even in small-town America. And in a work vehicle of all places. Perhaps that individual is just being foolish. Maybe it's small-town foolishness.

Do you think this happens to the "other guy?" If you leave your keys in your car you might become the "other guy." Don't be that guy. Don't leave your keys behind for teenagers to find, because at least in my experience, your shit will be gone.

There was a furniture store that sat near the edge of the small downtown where I grew up. I don't think I was ever in that store more than one time in my whole life, but with its large glass front windows, you could see a lot of the inventory so I felt familiar with the place. The furniture business had a delivery van, one of those elongated vans popular with carpet installers—long enough to hold a twelve-foot roll of carpet without sticking out the back, or a fifteen-foot roll poking out the rear lashed doors. It was red.

This story is also about a friend I had when I was a teenager. His name was Chad. Chad, whose main reason it seemed for existing was to facilitate debauchery. This story is as much about that red van as our protagonist, Chad. You could say the three main talking points are: Chad, the red van, and the grand theft auto.

Let's start with Chad. I can't confirm his name, but for the sake of this story let us just call him Chad, and say that his real name may or may not rhyme with "dad," or maybe "mad" is better. Chad had what would be characterized as an unhealthy living situation. When any of us stayed at his house, we understood that there was no curfew and no rules of any kind. Chad lived with his older brother and his grandmother, in a small house not far from the downtown area. It was an easy skateboard ride to town, which always made it a good staging area for our assault upon that area.

Looking back on Chad's behavior and persona, I can come up with no word other than unhinged. I know it's a strong word to hang on a teenager, but being around him, you felt he had no sense of danger, and little fear of, well, anything. If Chad had been able to purchase a Gatling gun, I could imagine him mounting it to his second-floor bedroom windowsill to mow down anyone in sight: man, woman, child, beast, friend, foe, Domino's Pizza delivery person, everyone. Years after the time in my life I spent in Chad's presence, a man named Shawn Nelson stole a Korean War-era Patton tank from the local National Guard Armory. He then went on a rampage, smashing everything he came across with the tank. Before I knew the name of the man who did this craziness, I was guessing it was Chad. Just seemed like the kind of thing he would do.

In retrospect, I can't honestly say I liked him very much. It was a relationship based purely on need. I needed a place to stay that had no rules to follow. I think he just needed someone to pal around with and assist him in his mayhem. Neither of us was the kind of friend all the others would ask about if we weren't around. We were never going to be the life of the party, and we enjoyed not having attention drawn to ourselves. In complete contradiction to this, Chad once participated in some sort of high school-sanctioned belching contest. Having lost, he proclaimed it to be rigged.

Now, to the grand theft auto problem. I have not attended law school and am mostly unfamiliar with the law, so sticking with that theme, I feel it is probably okay to tell this story. At least I know the furniture store that owned the red van is no longer in business. That storefront has changed hands quite a few times since all this happened. I'm sure the statute of limitations for felony car theft has worn off. Again, at least I think so.

I had heard from a mutual friend that Chad had been spending his nights of late joyriding in some bus he found the keys in. Now, this was not the summer, this was *during* the school year. Chad was doing this and still coming to school in the morning, mostly.

Chad wandered the city alone at night, searching for unlocked vehicles then once inside, he would look for keys to start them. If no keys were found, he would move on. I don't even think he was interested in anything that may have been inside the vehicle, just the keys.

The vehicle Chad had found unlocked and was able to start up and drive away with, strangely enough, was a bus. Not a take-the-kids-to-school school bus, but a bus that doubled for what was public transportation in our little town. It only operated within the city limits, and I grew up a few miles outside of that, so the bus was worthless to me. The style was more like what you would see shuttling drunken partygoers to-and-fro for bachelor and bachelorette parties.

This seemed insane, even for Chad. These buses were used during the day, and there was no good reason why one would be out at night, especially in the early morning, and out on country roads to boot. Remarkably, he got away with this more than once.

I was all for flouting the rule of law, but this seemed beyond my understanding of what kind of criminal activity I would be a part of. A small part of me thought it sounded fun. After a few nights, however, someone realized keys were being left in the bus, or that it was being taken out and driven at night because when Chad went back for another night of thievery, the keys were no longer inside. That bit of fun had run its course.

Chad, however, turned out to be a rather resourceful guy. Since he required little sleep to be both a car thief and a high school student, he was free to wander the streets of our hometown at night.

The full scope of Chad's misdeeds was unknown to all but him. We were all better off not knowing.

What Chad was doing wasn't theft for financial gain. He had no chop shop waiting to hand him cash for whatever clunker he was turning over; he simply wanted to find a vehicle for the night, smoke some weed, tear through the countryside, and then return it before the owner knew it was gone.

As it happens, not long after Chad's shuttle bus extravaganza came to an end, he came across a van, which as I mentioned before was used by a local furniture store. And more importantly, Chad found the keys inside. A rusty red delivery van *was* less conspicuous than a large shuttle bus being driven off hours. And so, the abuse of the red van began. I wasn't there for the inaugural, trip but it became the stuff of legend. Regaled with stories of fishtailing down dirt roads while stoned teens lay in the back being tossed around like ping pong balls inside of a lottery ball machine.

I reserved my seat for the next ride-along. The plan was for Chad by himself to pick up the van from the furniture store's rear parking, then pick up that night's guests, me included. We'd be picked up from a central location—this would fall onto the member of the group whose parents wouldn't notice three or four kids wander off at midnight, weren't home, or were half in the bag by midnight.

Chad did the work to get the vehicle, so he was essentially in charge. In charge of what, or who, was a mystery. No one had a driver's license, so it wasn't that fact that elevated Chad to ad hoc leader. He was mad enough to steal the thing, and so in turn would be the sole pilot on our outings. We would have to settle for being accomplices.

Chad commandeered the van and picked us up at midnight, weed was quickly smoked, and the van was steered out of town onto the backroads of Lenawee County, Michigan. The stories that found their way to me after the previous van outing was no exaggeration, as once Chad found his way onto the backroads, we were bounced around in the back of the van. The van was not designed to be a bounce house, so before the fun could wear off, someone was mildly injured by a rusty piece of sheet metal. The fun needed to end for the night, so Chad headed back into town and dropped us at our homes.

How often Chad took the van, only he knows. The story was that he would take it out alone every night. Just for kicks, maybe? Again, this was how he liked to operate. Chad didn't need or even care to get a pat on the back from those who considered him their friend for his theft. You were just a minor distraction from whatever grand plan he was working on at the moment. You may have been in on the spoils of the plan, but you were never actually on the planning committee, which consisted of just one person.

After a week or so, Chad had an epiphany. He could keep this scam going for a proposed indefinite amount of time. What he needed was his own set of keys to the van. Chad then hatched a plan to keep the keys overnight after returning the van to the parking lot where it was housed. He would then take the ignition key, get it copied, and return the keys to the van that evening, placing them in a location that would make the driver say, "Hey, there they are, I knew those keys were in here somewhere."

To me, this seemed like a keen little ruse. It was even plausible that the worker who entered the van in the morning would be a different person than the one who exited the van the previous day. Calls would be made, workers annoyed, the spare keys would be located, and life would move on. Chad's plan seemed to have a chance. Granted I was like fourteen at the time, so any plan which had the sum of more than two parts seemed like a good plan to me.

The whole mess Chad had created was a ticking time bomb, and anyone other than a fourteen-year-old kid should have realized it could not last much longer. He was so determined to flout the law, to take these joy rides in this shitty delivery van, that looking back at these events, I can't understand them, no matter how hard I try.

Chad put his plan into motion by stealing the keys, getting the ignition key copied, then returning the original set to the van. It was claimed to be a success. I felt that Chad took pride in his accomplishment, something that was undoubtedly rare in his life up to this point. In a perverted way, he now seemed to think he had part ownership of the van. Keys equaled ownership in his mind.

We tended to get around via skateboard at this point in our lives, but I lived too far out of town to skateboard into where my friends lived. Chad, on the other hand, lived the perfect distance from downtown for skateboarding. When most of us became obsessed with tricks and skate videos, Chad saw his skateboard as a tool. It got him out of his unhappy home and transported him into our unhappy little downtown; Chad would make this trip anytime, day or night.

A couple of nights after Chad swapped the keys, we all met at his place before skating downtown. A night of joy-riding was in store. We knew where the van was, and it was Chad's for the taking.

We skated downtown, slinking into the few dark recesses that were on offer. As we approached the parking lot where the van typically sat overnight, we picked up our boards and crept up to where the van should have been. It was gone. But where was it? Was the fun coming to an abrupt end? Chad was not giving up so easily.
"Let's skate around—maybe it's parked somewhere else," Chad called out.

So, we skated through nearby lots. We skated down the few alleyways our town possessed. And just as we were about to give up, there it was, parked nowhere near the store but in the back lot of a local Mexican restaurant. We stood for a moment in amazement when suddenly the word rang out, that all teenage rule-breakers feared, "Cops!"

The boards came down and we were off in the opposite direction fleeing the van and downtown.

"In here," I heard Chad call out.

He had been at my side, but as I spun my head around, he was peering into a dumpster that sat behind a neighboring law office. I skidded my board to a stop, jumped off, and ran back to the dumpster as Chad and the others were climbing over the side. I peeked over the side, and in the light of the buzzing dim overhead parking lot lights, it looked empty. I was glad it was trash day.

Once inside we all sat silent, panting, our backs against the walls of the dumpster, skateboards heaped in the middle as if we were about to use them for kindling. Several teens on skateboards don't just disappear into the night, and the local police department was quick to figure this out. All looking skyward out the top of the open dumpster, we could see headlights flashing by, then lingering on a nearby wall adjacent to the dumpster. The distinct sound of a police radio, followed by doors opening, then closing, filled us with dread. Dread turned to delight for a brief moment as I believed the officers were simply parking in the lot and were wandering off in search of us. Suddenly, a bright light as if from God above shone down upon the new residents of Waste Management Dumpster #C-1109, located in the rear of 102 S. Winter St. We stirred as if being woken up, in a dumpster, at midnight, with skateboards. "Come on out," rang God's voice from overhead.

We all clambered out of the dumpster with our boards and stood at attention. The police officer then turned his flashlight down into the dumpster, once again to make sure we didn't have a very small friend who was hiding in the stinky corner. His light fell upon something small and shiny I hadn't noticed when climbing out. It was the one and only thing left in that dumpster once we were out.

"Whose car keys are those?" came the officer's stern voice.

A chorus of mumbling denials was sent back his way.

"None of us is old enough to drive, sir."

"We've had reports of someone taking the Robertson's Furniture Van without permission" the officer lazily said turning from one to the next of us.

"None of us are old enough to drive, sir," was all anyone uttered in response to the officer's declaration.

"We were just out skateboarding." This time it was Chad who spoke up, and I could hear the contempt in his voice. It was like we all signed a legal document when entering the skateboarding world to have disdain for all police officers. They were our sworn enemies, no matter the circumstance.

As the officer took a moment to ponder the insolent juvenile skateboarders, and the amount of paperwork in his future for a simple act or curfew violation, it seemed some of us were about to catch a huge break, which I'm sure stemmed from a bit of laziness. The officer called another car to the scene to split us up and give us all a nice ride home. I pointed out to the officer closest to me that I was staying with Chad and needed to be taken to his home instead of my own. Without hesitation, Chad and I were put into one car and driven to his home, where his grandmother was awakened, given a brief speech about how Chad should be kept in at night, and the officer was off. Chad then refused to hear a single word from her and stomped off upstairs, me in tow. The first words out of his mouth after that were. "Do you think it's still there?"

"Maybe?" was the only reply I could manage. I could recognize our good fortune, even if he couldn't.

I was taken aback by Chad's boldness and single-mindedness. That van key symbolized something meaningful to Chad. But what? Did the police take Chad's storybook happy ending away? More likely, Chad was a child, kicking and screaming from having his toy taken away.

We let the subject die, both us of thankful for the bullet we'd dodged that night. This would spell the end of my being part of the auto-theft crew. It was too much risk for me and too high of stakes. When that comment came from Chad, I also realized he might not stop, and the following nights would see him back downtown searching for cars to boost.

I distanced myself from him after that night. We once shared a locker in high school, but an unprovoked altercation in between classes ended that chapter in our friendship too. When Chad reached the age where he could quit school, he did. He had no intention of spending one more minute in high school than was acceptable to him.

Until this time in my life popped into my head, I hadn't given Chad any thought in many years. Not the stealing of the van, not the way he would order a hamburger at McDonald's minus the patty, not the way he would stare off into the void like he was in power save mode, and not the fact that his soulless existence, which I believed would haunt me forever, never actually made a ripple in the timeline of my life. All his friends forgot him—they just moved on, grew up, stopped yelling at their grandmother, and embraced adulthood. Chad will always be chasing the red van. Chasing that thing that is over the horizon, just out of reach.

Will Thirteen People Fit on a Bus?

Now that I am old enough to be considered over the hill, I often find my head is jam-packed. There's no better way to describe the feeling. It's the combination of worry, dread, hope, loss, optimism, regret, determination, doubt, drunkenness, and sometimes even a little happiness that sneaks in. I haven't found a good system of organization for all of that. I've been told meditation could help, but no time has been spent investigating how specifically it could help. Drugs, I hear, are another answer. Some people use marijuana, and there are even folks who have taken to microdosing psychedelics as a means of organizing their minds.

Could psychedelics help me organize my life? When I was younger, taking psychedelics would end up costing me six to eight hours of a day, staring at walls, sitting in an empty bathtub, wandering around fields talking to the wheat, or meandering around a construction site, destined to snag my shirt on rebar or step on a nail.

Nothing profound germinated to come out later as a legitimate thought. Incoherent babble, and pointing out the blatantly obvious, was the norm after ingesting the drug. It would all seem too profound at the time, the drug binding to receptors in the brain, causing hallucinations, and again causing utter bullshit to be spewed from you and all your friends.

On one occasion, my dear friend Tom took a dose of LSD and then became fixated on a fictitious bus being on its way and where all the people would fit once the bus arrived. Now, thirteen people were the specific number of folks Tom was concerned with finding seats for. But would they all fit? If you had more than thirteen people, where would the excess go?

At times, I've wondered if people still use larger doses of LSD and if conversations like this occur weekly, somewhere—a fixation upon which their lives would seemingly hang in the balance. This life-and-death struggle to come to terms with why rocks are shaped differently, why we keep going to see Batman moves even though those who are creating the movies keep changing the person who plays Batman, how if you had a pen and paper you could write the best song/novel/poem ever, and how when thirteen people show up you're going to need to find a bus to put them all in.

LSD never made me see the boogie man. It never allowed me the ability to tap into some previously unknown potential, and it certainly never drove me to write the greatest song ever. It seemed like a distraction from the doldrums I found living my life, inside and outside the home. I was allowed to escape my poor family life, my failing grades at school, my lack of friends, the girl I loved who didn't know I existed, and the negative moral debt I couldn't seem to stop accumulating.

How would an LSD trip suit me as an adult? The worry is I've grown too uptight to allow myself this briefest of escapes. Sadly, my friend Tom is no longer with us to re-ponder where these hypothetical thirteen people will go once they've arrived. Tom could have been my guide along our six-to-eight-hour journey. There's little doubt he would have been game.

These days, I feel like I don't need *that* kind of break from my life, but things can change, quickly. Maybe microdosing is the answer for me: small doses in which I can work on my internal organizing. And maybe, just maybe, I can answer that most important question: will thirteen people fit on a bus, and if not, where will they go?

Do *You* Get It?

I was attending this poker party a couple of decades ago. A friendly little game, hosted by a guy I met at work. One night, one of the regulars said he had a joke. Here it is.

A woman walked up to me in a bar and said:

"Excuse me, are you Rick?"

"No," I said, "my name is Rich."

Looking a little puzzled, the woman replied, "I was supposed to meet a guy named Rick here tonight for a date, my name is Candy."

"Weird," I replied, "I'm supposed to meet someone here named Brandy."

"Brandy?" the woman again said, puzzled.

"Yeah, Brandy, with a B," I said confidently.

The woman then turned to the bartender and said, "Excuse me, can I get a deer?"

This was the joke. The other guys all laughed, and honestly, I still don't get it. Were both people dyslexic? I mean, that's not funny, is it? Making fun of people with dyslexia? Or were they just stupid? I guess it might be okay to make fun of them for being stupid. Hell, maybe I wasn't listening properly when the guy told the joke.

The Bully

Throughout elementary, middle, and high school, I was fortunate enough never to fall victim to bullying, nor was I the bully. I wasn't the fastest, the cleverest, or the coolest kid in school. I was a skinny kid with just enough of everything and had enough friends that bullying me wasn't worth it.

Bullying a kid with an unidentified number of friends *and* uncertain popularity could cause a little retribution misdirection. Who would come to my aid: teachers? Friends? Older siblings? A local drug dealer?

There were rumors I was friends with a kid named Jason Baker. Unverified stories of him smoking Marlboro Reds and carrying a knife all by the fifth-grade grade swirled around that kid. Jason and I *did* know each other, and we met under strange circumstances. He was going up to all the kids in our sixth-grade class, asking if our parents smoked. Well, one of mine did. Jason asked me if I could swipe a lighter that night and bring it to him the next day. Seemed like good Karma to me, so I did. The following morning, as I was walking down the hall, I heard someone calling my name. All anyone knew was that Jason and I had a pleasant exchange, and everyone saw him patting me on the back, and smiling.

What I gave Jason was a plain silver Zippo lighter. It had been sitting around the house for ages and was never in use. I think it was my dad's backup for his backup. I seem to recall my dad saying, "I stole it from that asshole Jerry at work."

There were also the Jaimez twins, Roy and Raymond. They were the stuff of legend. One of the tales goes like this: An upper-class student caught one of the Jaimez twins (Raymond) in the bathroom. The upper-class student was mistaken though, as

Roy was hiding in one of the stalls and simply let the older student believe he had Raymond cornered. Before the older student could lay a finger on Raymond, Roy burst out of the stall at a full run, and both brothers kicked this older student in the balls at the same time. While the student lay writhing on the bathroom floor in agony, the twins spent a full minute rubbing soap into the dude's eyes. Then, if that wasn't bad enough, they pissed on him. No one dared fuck with the Jaimez twins after that day. The older student ended up switching schools and no one heard from him again. Some say he might have gone blind from the cheap-ass soap used in school bathrooms.

It was true I knew the twins, and we'd hung out when we were little. The twins and I were nothing more than casual acquaintances by high school, but our moms were still friends, and man did those Jaimez twins love their mama. The only person they'd listen to.

Of course, I wasn't immune to all violence during my school years. In tenth grade, I was approached by a guy who took umbrage with me regarding some girl he liked. I don't recall all the circumstances, but some night he saw me riding my skateboard, jumped out of his car, and slugged me. It seemed too random, looking back.

Another incident happened in my junior year of high school. There was a guy named Jose, who seemed too big and too old to be high-school-aged. It happened to be my junior year, but he was in his second senior year. Old enough to drink in Canada, probably. Jose's schtick was to walk up to some kid during the school day and inform them that unfortunately, they were chosen to meet him at the edge of the woods a short walk from school, promptly at 2:55 that day for a rousing round of fisticuffs.

I heard this had happened on several occasions but typically involved some of the tougher kids in school, whom Jose wanted to put in their place. Jose and the other kid would scuffle, and then would both be suspended for a short time, leaving Jose to return to school, and find another victim. Great system, eh?

As I mentioned before, I shared a class with Jose, who was in attendance about as much as I was, so we rarely crossed paths. I doubt he even knew my name, until the day *I* slipped into Jose's radar and lost "fight roulette." On his way to his seat, he stopped at my desk to inform me that yes, indeed, it was my turn, and I would need to meet him on the edge of those same woods for another exciting game of bare-knuckle brawling. He then walked calmly over to his seat, which was several rows behind mine. *What the fuck just happened*? I wondered.

I sat frozen, and confused, all the while weighing the options in my head. I didn't like school anyway—I could just leave and not come back. Then a quiet voice drifted up from behind. A familiar, kind voice.

"What did Jose say to you?" It was my friend Heather, who sat directly behind me in class. "Did he say he wanted to fight you after school?"

I nodded my confirmation. Through my haze, I could hear Heather whispering to the *other* Heather, and then to another friend of ours, Angie. Only whispers.

Then loud voices cut through the hazy visions of me being tracked down by Jose.
"How dare you threaten him? He hasn't done anything to you!"
"If you want to fight him, you'll have to fight all of us too."

It was my female friends, coming to my rescue. Jose had met his match. No matter how tough or how badly he wanted to be atop that fighter's ranking, there was no way he was going to agree to fight four people, three of them female. Knowing he was beaten, he took the only way out he could. Jose got up from his seat, walked over to me, and put his hand on my shoulder. My haze thickened.

"I was just kidding man," he told me. "Just a joke."

He then patted my shoulder and went back to his seat, and we never exchanged another word. If you want to get technical, I never did speak one word to him. Jose *wasn't* joking, but thankfully my friends came to my rescue. In a matter of sixty seconds, I had gone from Jose's easy target to a complete pain in the ass for him. His hasty retreat had been warranted. My dear friends the Jaimez brothers were long gone, doing a stint in the juvenile detention center for a string of robberies around town. Maybe Jose knew they were my muscle, so to speak.

Jose didn't last much longer in school, nor did I. Our exit strategies, while different, were both effective. At the end of the day, Jose and I might have had more in common than we both knew. Our love of the Bee Gees? Probably not. It was our silent pact. A pact made up of our mutual disdain for the authority over us, provided by the educational system.

No Peeking

I dated this girl who used to watch me sleep. It was unnerving waking up to someone lying on their side next to you, just watching you. Watching. Staring. Boring holes into my not-entirely-handsome face.

Honestly, I'm not Michelangelo's David. I have not been approached to model for a store, magazine, etc. What I have repeatedly been told is I appear quite dead while asleep. Was she worried about me? That I would stop breathing?

Fires are meant to be ogled at. Okay, let me clarify that remark. Small, *controlled* fires are meant to be ogled at. As in, one inside a backyard fire pit, or your fireplace. Not a house in Detroit, or the god damned forest.

Folks also go to car races, mostly to see the crashes. What's the equivalent here? Maybe night-terrors?

On a trip with my friend Dave, we sat down by the Dublin Docklands, smoking and staring at the water. Smoking. Staring. Smoking. And after forty-five minutes, it got old, so we wandered off to find something else to do. *That* is more exciting than watching me sleep.

In my home in Ann Arbor, I had the wood-burning fireplace converted to gas. I don't live near Sherwood Forest, so acquiring wood would have been a pain in the ass. And a fake fire in a fireplace is just as good in my opinion. All the fun without the cleanup.

Have you ever looked at a child while they are watching television? There is nothing else in the world that matters to them. The house could be burning down, and confederate soldiers could be kicking in your front door, and the kid would never know. Nor, am I a television.

A mutual friend of ours told me many years after we'd broken up that she had my face put on one of those big body pillows and she slept with it every night. The truth is, I have one of those too. It's fantastic!

A Rock and Roll Fantasy

I've played music for a good chunk of my life. Not professionally mind you. I feel it's important to set that tone early. I've been on stage more times than I can count. Mostly, small stages, mind you. I have vivid memories of ending a song and hearing one person clapping, the bartender. So, let me sum up all my years of playing in a single paragraph.

Rock and roll never got me laid. It never got me into a hip club for free. It cost me thousands of dollars. It did get me free drinks a couple of times if we're counting coffee. I have never signed an autograph on a scrap piece of paper, a woman's breast, or a man's bare chest. And the only person to ever take my picture while I was on stage was either a family member or a woman I was dating. Now *that* is a rock and roll life folks. Sign you up?

Default Optimism

For a while now, I have been too optimistic. Okay, maybe it's been forever. As I'm crashing my off-road bike into the trees and brush at a high rate of speed I'm thinking: this is strange, how did this happen? To me of all people?

When my friend played a trick on me when I was seventeen, which made me think I won the lotto, I believed him. I mean, why wouldn't I? After a few minutes of letting me believe I'd become instantly rich, he informed me that I did not win the lotto and it was all an elaborate joke. But, how could that be? Winning millions sure seemed like the kind of thing that would happen to *me*. It's me!

I don't go to the casinos and have big windfalls; I tend not to gamble at all. Other than my phantom lotto win, I've never even played. I would work with people who would all pool resources and buy tickets when the jackpot was getting to a couple of hundred million dollars, but I never participated.

 Years ago, I was on a date and said, "You know, I'm a pretty lucky guy."
To which she replied, "Yes, but aren't you divorced?"

She *did* have a point, but I've never added being lucky in love to this default optimism I have.

I had a roommate at one point in time named Markus. I would describe Markus this way: you know the guy who sits in the same chair that you were just in, but when he sits in it, the chair collapses into a heap of sticks? That's Markus.

I've always looked at luck (for lack of a better term) in life like a storm cloud. You can do your best to avoid the storm, but eventually, there's no outrunning it. You'll get hit.

Yes, I've come out to my car in a busy parking lot to find a dent in the door, but these things are easily fixed.

Yes, if the power goes out in my house, I assume I am not alone and it will eventually come back on.

Yes, I believe my paycheck will come in this Friday, and when my yearly review rolls around, my boss will tell me I am doing a good job. Why wouldn't he?

Yes, if a crazy man is elected President of the United States, I just shrug it off and I'll just vote again in a few years, for the other guy. Again.

Yes, if I drop something heavy on my foot or tear off my toenail from kicking the bed leg, I know it will heal. Of course, it will.

The sun will rise.

The store will have milk, eggs, and bread.

If my wife finds someone else, I'll be okay, and at some point down the road, I will find someone else, though as I mentioned before, this kind of luck could be riding on a whole different set of storm clouds.

When Wendy's fucks up my order, it will still be something I want to eat.

If it's cloudy tonight and I cannot see the stars, it's okay, they'll be back soon.

Perhaps you're wondering if I am full of shit? Or where this kind of optimism comes from? It's a good question, to which I do not know the answer. Maybe I am full of shit? Maybe I'm a white male fortunate enough not to have been born into a dreadful situation, like extreme poverty, or abuse.

Could it be that I have always believed we create our world, and if built well enough we could buy ourselves a fucking big umbrella, which would protect us from just about everything?

I'm no different, no cleverer. This is the play I've constructed from rules I was handed at birth. Sure, there are times I've just jerked the wheel in a particular direction and it's not killed me. I *do* try and limit those, though.

So, if I did create this, how did I do it? Is this something I can market? I don't see why not. Can you teach this, or has it been handed down by someone? This couldn't possibly be genetic, could it? Again, can I market, box, and sell this?

The only conclusion that you (the reader) can come to is that this is white male privilege. Being white and male, how does someone recognize that some privilege has been set in motion generations before? Maybe privilege is arbitrary? But being a white male, aren't I making the argument in saying privilege is arbitrary? Shit, I'm going in circles here, aren't I?

What about this: this subject of which I speak should only be glanced at, and never properly studied. White male privilege can and should be studied, but never my crazy luck—storm cloud theory. Go ahead and stand at the shoreline and guess how deep the water is. But, only guess. *Never* get in. Did you catch that?
Water = my crazy theory.

Depth of water = researching my theory.

Let me leave you with this. You rent a boat and take it out to the middle of your white-male-privileged lake. Let's not get hung up on the kind of boat here. Your boat begins to sink, and you attempt to call for help via the ship's radio. You are then electrocuted by the very thing you believed could save you. You die one shitty death. Your wife will find someone else, you'll still receive your paycheck (albeit only one more), and the great Wendy's in the sky will still fuck up your order.

Get it? Can you sift through to see a metaphor? No, I didn't think so. I'd be worried if you could.

Shit happens. Stay positive. Don't buy a boat.

About the Author

Bradley Poore, is the author of *A JOURNEY TO THE MIDDLE: How I embraced mediocrity and failed to turn my old vacuum into a rocket ship. Men of War* is his second book of essays. Bradley is considered by many to be a fool's fool; with very little understanding or knowledge of how the world works.

He loves waffle fries, chainsaw sculptures, traveling by train, and the Amish. Bradley lives in Ann Arbor, MI.